THE MYSTERY OF THE INDEFATIGABLE INK

THE THREE INVESTIGATORS

IN

THE MYSTERY OF THE INDEFATIGABLE INK

BY

ELIZABETH ARTHUR
& STEVEN BAUER

BASED ON CHARACTERS
CREATED BY ROBERT ARTHUR

Hollow Tree Press 2025

A HOLLOW TREE PRESS BOOK

Copyright © 2025
Elizabeth Arthur and Steven Bauer
Hollow Tree Press LLC

Jacket Concept Elizabeth Arthur
Jacket Design and Cover Art
© 2025 Hollow Tree Press LLC
Cover Art Pashur House

"The Three Investigators" ® & "???" ®
By Permission of Elizabeth Arthur

Published in the United States of America
All Rights Reserved

ISBN PB: 978-1-965321-24-9
ISBN HC: 978-1-965321-25-6
ISBN EB: 978-1-965321-26-3

CONTENTS

1

Jupiter Has His Work Cut Out For Him

The downtown shopping area was quiet as Jupiter Jones chained his bike to a parking meter outside Miles Hardware. Rocky Beach was a sleepy town on summer mornings, and though the day had barely started, it was already beginning to heat up. The sun spilled over the mountains to the east and splashed down on the small town's main street. Most of the storefronts hadn't yet opened, but Mr. Szabó, who Jupiter had known ever since he was a boy, welcomed his customers at 8 a.m. almost every day of the year.

Jupiter stood for a moment and surveyed his hometown. It had changed a bit since he was young, but it was still the same in many ways – welcoming to people from all over the world, a place of kindness and sanity. He was proud of Rocky Beach, and he was also glad to be back, after a Three Investigators case which had not only taken him to the city of Santa Barbara but had also brought him up against a peculiarly sinister set of villains.

A Greek man who had once worked for

the Greece Ministry of Culture had gotten together with an American man who worked for
Immigration and Customs Enforcement, and
the results might have been disastrous. That
they hadn't been had been due to hard work,
clear thought, and a measure of luck on the
part of Jupiter, Bob Andrews, Pete Crenshaw,
and Mallory MacLeod – and also to the intui-
tions of their friend Rafael Solares.

But while the story of The Three Investigators' triumph had been splashed in papers all
over California – and even in other parts of the
United States – and the Greek government was
giving them a Certificate of Appreciation as
well as an honorarium, for Jupiter the triumph
had been muted. The older he got, and the
more cases he and his friends had solved, the
more aware he'd become that people he'd assumed, when he was younger, were honest and
trustworthy frequently weren't.

Of course, to some extent, he had always known that. If he hadn't, he would hardly
have founded an investigative firm when he was
only twelve years old. But the last case had
really brought it home to him.

However, at the moment, he was heading for Miles Hardware on a very domestic
mission for his Aunt Mathilda, who – together

with his uncle Titus Jones – owned and operated the Jones Salvage Yard, behind which was the house in which Jupiter had lived since he was a baby. You'd think that with all the tools the Jones Salvage Yard had collected over the years – tools piled in boxes, displayed on shelves in sheds, and still unsold – Aunt Mathilda would already have a pipe cutter in her possession.

But at breakfast that morning she had been quite stern.

"Jupiter," she'd said. "You and your friends have been gallivanting all over this great state for the past weeks – up in Napa, over to Santa Barbara. Land sakes, you'd think you had ants in your pants! I expect you'll settle down for a time now?"

Jupiter shook his head doubtfully. "Perhaps," he said. "Though we never know where our next case will come from."

"Your next case is to bike downtown and get me a pipe cutter," she said, "so that I can size my new curtain rods properly. Yesterday, Mallory discovered an excellent set, complete with finials, that Titus had hidden in a shed. You know I've wanted to make new curtains for the living room for some time, and now I'm going to! After I do, you can take down all the old rods and put up the new ones."

Jupiter looked at his uncle.

"Don't look at me, Jupiter," Titus Jones said. "I've got my own list."

"And Mallory will finally be back at work!" Aunt Mathilda said. "She has a backlog. She hasn't even finished inventorying all the things Titus brought back from the Napa Valley."

Mallory was The Three Investigators' Special Consultant. She'd moved to Rocky Beach from Scotland the previous summer after her Scottish father had died, and she'd become an integral part of the team.

Aunt Mathilda's voice softened as she sat down in her chair, cupping her hands around her coffee. "It's not that I'm not proud of the four of you." She meant Pete and Bob, as well as Jupiter and Mallory. "Heavens to Betsy! You've certainly started out this summer with a bang. Both cases in the papers − and not only in Rocky Beach, but in Los Angeles! Still, I don't want this going to your head. You can do a few errands for a helpless old lady, can't you?"

Jupiter groaned. "You're not an old lady," he had said decisively. "And you're certainly not helpless."

"I know that!" Aunt Mathilda had said. "So you'll go right away and get the pipe cutter?"

Jupiter smiled, remembering the conversation. As a matter of fact, he agreed with his aunt that it would be great if their next case took place right here in Rocky Beach. While he wouldn't call what The Three Investigators had been doing ever since school let out for the summer "gallivanting," it was nice to be home again, and he wouldn't mind staying home for a while.

As he opened the door of Miles Hardware, the bell jingled, and he stood inside in the dimness, waiting for his eyes to adjust. It was a real old-fashioned hardware store, filled with rows of shelves, each one stuffed from bottom to top with gadgets, hand tools and power tools, nails and screws of all descriptions and sizes, keys and locks and hinges, and plumbing and electrical fixtures.

It hadn't changed much at all since Jupiter's first visit with his uncle many years before. The overhead fluorescent lights flickered, and the store smelled of worn wood and machine oil, paint and the tang of metal. Uncle Titus had often said that Mr. Szabó had at least one of everything in the known universe for sale —

and that he would never shop anywhere else.

"Jupiter," Mr. Szabó called as he emerged from the murkiness of one of the aisles. "So good to see you! You're up early."

Mr. Szabó was in his mid-fifties with a hawklike nose and jet-black hair. He was wearing a gray apron, and a green plastic visor jutted out over his sharp eyes. But he was moving slowly and his voice sounded tired and gloomy. His usually animated face looked slack and his hands hung at his sides. He was clearly depressed.

"Good morning, Mr. Szabó," Jupiter said. "How are you?"

"Ugh," Mr. Szabó said, shaking his head from side to side. "I don't want to talk about it. What can I do for you?"

"My aunt sent me to buy a pipe cutter," Jupiter said. "She wants to shorten some old curtain rods."

Mr. Szabó nodded. "Right this way."

Now that he had a task, he walked more briskly and Jupiter followed him down a long aisle that teemed with plumbing supplies – chrome and copper and PVC piping, elbows and sink traps.

"Here you go," Mr. Szabó said, pausing about halfway down. He picked up a small gadget. "You fasten this on the pipe where you want to cut and then you push down on the scribe and go around and around until the pipe breaks! I have three different kinds. You can choose whichever you want." He seemed happy to help, and to have such a variety.

As Jupiter examined the various choices, Mr. Szabó stood nearby with his hands crossed on his chest. "I read in the paper about you and your friends," he said. "You're making quite a name for yourselves. The Three Investigators! Your aunt and uncle must be so proud of how well you're doing."

"Thank you," Jupiter said, unexpectedly pleased by this remark.

"If only things were going so well for me," Mr. Szabó said gloomily.

"What's the matter?" Jupiter asked. He had chosen the pipe cutter he thought would work best and now gave his full attention to Mr. Szabó.

The man shook his head in discouragement. "I'm sure you can guess that business has been down, with all the competition online. People used to come and ask for my help, but now they just stay home and order by computer."

"But no online store can offer the years

of experience you have," Jupiter said. He suddenly felt guilty, because even he had ordered online from time to time. It had seemed so effortless.

"Tell that to my ex-customers!" Mr. Szabó said. "Your own aunt and uncle must feel the pinch, too. And now there is this terrible Congressman, Douglas Clark, who went off to Washington and managed to get even more taxes and regulations put on small businesses like Miles Hardware and the Jones Salvage Yard. I have always worked very hard, but in the last few years I've spent more time keeping up with all the new rules than I have taking care of my store. I understand with big companies that try to get away with things. But a small business like mine!"

Jupiter winced. Mr. Szabó clearly did not know that, with Mallory's help, the Jones Salvage Yard was now doing a healthy online business.

"Yes," Jupiter said weakly – though, to tell the truth, he had sometimes heard his uncle complain about the taxes and regulations, too. Mr. Szabó put the pipe cutter in a small paper bag and pushed it across the counter at Jupiter.

"That will be $17.97. With tax." He sighed. "To tell you the truth, I'm a whisker away from shutting down Miles Hardware."

"I'm very sorry to hear that," Jupiter said. He was. He was also shocked. Miles Hardware had been a mainstay on the main street of Rocky Beach his whole life. "Is there anything I can do to help?" he asked.

"That is very kind of you, Jupiter," Mr. Szabó said. "But there is not much that anyone can do. Things are just getting worse all the time. I am sorry for dragging you into my troubles, but it has been very much on my mind."

"I'm sure it has," Jupiter said.

"Maybe you do not know my story," Mr. Szabó said. "My parents came to California in 1956 from Hungary. They lived in a small town near the border with Austria, and when Soviet troops came into the country with their tanks and their guns, my parents were able to take what they could carry and flee into Austria. In Vienna they got help, and they came to the United States. I was born here, ten years later, and my parents raised me to love what America stood for. My real name is Milan, but I changed it to Miles."

Jupiter was amazed to hear all this. He'd not known much of anything about Mr. Szabó's history, even though he'd known the man since he was four or five years old. He was also astonished to realize that, with his own Serbian background, he and Mr. Szabó had something very real in common. Their relatives had both had to suffer under repressive political regimes.

"But now," Mr. Szabó said, sighing. "What is happening to America? Giving people too much power over others almost always leads the people in power to abuse it. And the people who write about the people in power – the so-called 'journalists' – are almost as bad as they are!"

The bell over the front door jangled and Jupiter turned to see an older woman walk in. She was in her seventies, Jupiter thought, and her long gray hair was piled tidily upon her head. She walked with a slight limp and she carried a cane, but it looked to Jupiter as though she could just as easily use it as a weapon if she needed to. She looked like someone who did not suffer fools gladly.

"Good morning, Annika," Mr. Szabó said. "I will be with you in just a moment. I was just telling this young man about my parents leaving Hungary. Let me introduce you. Annika, this is Jupiter Jones. Jupiter, this is Mrs. Annika Vasiliev. We have known each other a long time," Mr. Szabó said to Jupiter. "My parents and Annika are fellow émigrés." He gestured toward the old woman. "Tell Jupiter your story."

Mrs. Vasiliev seemed a bit taken aback by this invitation.

"It's an old story, Miles," she said, "and my mind is on other things right now." She swatted the air with her free hand, as if warding off bad thoughts. "A young friend of mine – he is a musician, in his early twenties, Ivan Fedorov, very talented, and such a good-hearted young man. He has just gotten his first real break, and now that is in danger. He comes from a famous family – at least they are famous to me and those my age!"

Jupiter nodded politely, though the name was not familiar. "What seems to be the problem?" he asked.

"Ivan has written a wonderful song for a new movie about Catherine the Great," Mrs. Vasiliev said. "Both the music and the words. The song is the most important in the movie, and when it comes out, I know it will make him famous."

Jupiter was puzzled. There seemed to be no problem at all.

"But this horrible young man he went to

high school with is threatening to sue him! He claims Ivan stole both the melody and the words, and if he brings a lawsuit, the director has said he may have to abandon Ivan's song because he doesn't want bad publicity for his film."

Mrs. Vasiliev looked quite angry. "I have known Ivan since he was little," she said, "and he would never ever have stolen anything! He is a true artist, and very sensitive, and although he has hired a lawyer, the whole thing makes him very upset."

Jupiter didn't know what to say, but suddenly Mr. Szabó spoke again.

"I should have told you!" he said. "Jupiter and a number of his friends investigate things. They are called The Three Investigators, and they are becoming more and more famous every week! This summer alone they have already solved two big cases – including the robbery of those ancient Greek treasures from the museum up in Santa Barbara. It was in all the papers. Maybe they can help your friend!"

The expression on Mrs. Vasiliev's face changed. She suddenly looked very interested in Jupiter. "I read those articles," she said. "That was you, young man?"

"And my friends," Jupiter said, embarrassed. "It wasn't all me."

"My husband and I came to California from the Soviet Union in the early 1980s" she said, fixing him with a penetrating gaze. "My young friend is the grandson of the famous Vadim Fedorov. I met the family because Vadim was very involved with the group that sponsored Sasha and me when we first came to this country. The Soviet Union's borders were locked tight for many years after the 1917 revolution, but between 1960 and the time the Soviet Union fell apart, more than a quarter of a million Soviet Jews like me and Sasha were allowed to emigrate."

Jupiter had not heard of Vadim Fedorov, and from the expression on Annika Vasiliev's face, he was sure that he should have. But while Jupiter felt sorry for his grandson, Ivan, the case itself didn't sound all that exciting or intriguing, and besides, it was very hard to prove that someone hadn't done something – much harder than proving that he had!

Still, The Three Investigators' motto was "We Investigate Anything," and they were between cases at the moment. He'd already been hoping to get a case that kept them in and around Rocky Beach, Jupiter thought. In addition, Mrs. Vasiliev seemed truly agitated at what was happening to her friend, and he liked her, so he took out his wallet and handed her one of The Three Investigators' business cards.

"We'll be happy to look into this," he said, "if you can arrange to introduce us to Ivan Fedorov."

Mrs. Vasiliev took the card and looked at it with real interest.

Jupiter cleared his throat. "We actually have a fourth member – Mallory MacLeod, who's a Special Consultant – but her name isn't on the card yet."

Mrs. Vasiliev's eyes were bright. "Very good," she said. "Very, very good! I live right here in Rocky Beach and I can invite Ivan and his wife Cassandra to come to my apartment tomorrow, if you four could arrange to meet them then."

She took a pencil and a small notepad from her purse and wrote something down on a slip of paper before handing it to Jupiter. "Here is my address and phone number."

Jupiter glanced at the address and noticed that it was within biking distance of the Salvage Yard before folding the paper and putting it in his wallet for safekeeping.

"We'll ride our bikes to your place," he

said. "When would be a good time?"

"I'll call you," Mrs. Vasiliev said, "as soon as I've contacted Ivan and Cassandra."

Jupiter shook her hand gravely. "That will be fine," he said. "We'll see you tomorrow. Goodbye, Mr. Szabó. I'm sorry for your troubles."

Jupiter's aunt and uncle were on the front steps of the Office when he pulled through the wrought-iron gates of the Salvage Yard. Aunt Mathilda was shading her eyes against the morning glare.

"Land sakes!" she called. "Where have you been? I was starting to get worried."

Jupiter got off his bike and handed her the paper bag with the pipe cutter. "I wound up having an interesting conversation," he said. "Did you know that Mr. Szabó's parents got out of Hungary just as the Soviet Union invaded it with tanks?"

"Why, yes," Aunt Mathilda said, looking at Titus, who nodded. "I think we did know that about Miles."

"His real name is Milan," Jupiter said. "He changed it to Miles to sound more American, I think. I also met a woman who emigrated from the Soviet Union. I imagine they became friends because they both understood what life is like under repressive political regimes."

"How on earth did a topic like that come up?" Aunt Mathilda asked.

Jupiter had to think for a moment. "It all began with Mr. Szabó telling me about a Congressman named Douglas Clark. He said Clark was trying to pass legislation making it even harder for small business owners to compete. More rules, regulations, and taxes. He wondered if you and Uncle Titus were bothered by the same thing."

"I would say so!" Aunt Mathilda said. "If it weren't for Mallory, who knows what might be happening to us? Her descriptions on the new website have saved us. We've had a lot of new customers, and that's managed to make up for the money we've lost because of all the new rules and regulations. And paperwork! Do you remember the hoops we had to jump through to get Leif and Magnus hired and onto the payroll?" She snorted. "What do you think I do in this office all day? Read romance novels?"

"No," Jupiter said – though the thought of it made him smile. He hadn't really been aware of how much paperwork his aunt had had to do.

"It's no wonder that Miles is upset," Aunt Mathilda said. "It's lucky for us that we have a special niche in the marketplace. Most of our goods are unique. But little hardware stores and pharmacies and other shops that sell things you can buy online or at any big box store are in real trouble. They have less stock and have to charge higher prices. It's almost impossible for them to compete."

"I actually met that Douglas Clark once," Uncle Titus said. "I cannot recall anyone I disliked so much."

Coming from Uncle Titus – who was as good-natured as a human being could be, and who liked everybody – this was quite damning, Jupiter thought.

"No bones in his whole skeleton," Uncle Titus said. "Just Jell-O! So condescending and arrogant – ready to spend my money and then tell me what to do. The exact opposite of who should be in government."

"Who should be in government?" Jupiter asked.

His uncle laughed. "Someone who keeps his nose out of your business," Uncle Titus said. "Someone who remembers what my high school history teacher called the immutable ideal America was founded on. That idea being freedom, of course − to do, to speak, and to think. I'm a grown man, and I can make my own decisions. People need to be responsible for themselves."

Aunt Mathilda had taken the pipe cutter out of the bag. "Are you done, Titus?" she asked. "May I have my soap box back?"

"Certainly, my dear," Uncle Titus said. "And may I take this opportunity to tell you that you look smashing standing on it?"

Aunt Mathilda laughed. "Titus, you old flirt," she said. She wagged her finger at her nephew. "Jupiter, you could do worse than to study your uncle if you want to succeed with the ladies."

It wasn't something Jupiter thought about very often. But he smiled at his aunt's sudden good humor. Both his aunt and his uncle were blessed with very cheerful dispositions, while he himself ran to the more ruminative and occasionally melancholy. He thought − and not for the first time − that if the Joneses had ever had a son of their own, he probably would have been a lot like Pete.

"And thank you for this," Aunt Mathilda said as she examined the pipe cutter. "This will be perfect. As soon as I get the new curtain rods cut to the proper length and the new curtains made, you can help me by putting them up. After you take down the old ones. You certainly have your work cut out for you."

Jupiter nodded, a bit reluctantly, then asked if Mallory was there yet.

"She certainly is," Aunt Mathilda said. "And I'm finally getting a good day's work out of her. Now don't you go bothering her and throwing her off."

"I won't," Jupiter said. "I just need to speak to her."

Aunt Mathilda stopped bristling. Jupiter knew she had a soft spot for Mallory, and not just because she was such a good and handy worker.

"Do you know where she is?" he asked.

"She's in her favorite shed," Aunt Mathilda said. "The one with the little kitchen and the sofa. She's been turning it into her own office, bit by bit. Not that I blame her."

"Thanks," Jupiter said. "And don't worry. I won't interrupt her for long."

"You run along then," Aunt Mathilda said. "Go on. After all, she is a very pretty girl. And also a very smart one. Smart enough to know where the phrase 'have your work cut out for you' comes from. Which I bet you don't."

His aunt's expression was triumphant.

At that moment, he wished more than anything that he could tell his aunt she was wrong.

Unfortunately, he couldn't.

And because he always wanted to fill in the gaps in his knowledge as soon as he reasonably could, he decided to take a short detour to Headquarters and the computer on its old battered desk. When he got there, he realized, to his own surprise, that he was actually feeling a lot gloomier than he had realized. His dejection was deepened by how crowded and dingy the old mobile home trailer seemed.

Although it was true, in a way, that he was glad to be back in Rocky Beach, it was also true that their last two cases had been thrill rides. Both of them had brought The Three Investigators a lot of what Bob's father, a reporter, called "ink" – by which he meant a lot of coverage in the press. But the cases had also put him and his friends in contact with genuine ancient treasures. It was going to be a bit hard to recalibrate from the treasures, the triumph, and the recognition. More than a bit hard, maybe.

At the desk, he pushed aside a pile of books and papers and booted up the computer. After typing in "derivation of 'work cut out for you"'" he discovered that the expression came from sewing. From tailors and seamstresses, in the days when clothing was made by hand. Each item of clothing would have a pattern, and the process would start with someone cutting out all the individual parts from a piece of cloth before beginning to sew them together. When all the pieces had been assembled, the tailors or seamstresses had their work cut out for them.

It sounded remarkably restful, actually. To Jupiter, anyway. At least right at the moment. Because when your work *wasn't* cut out for you in advance (the way The Three Investigators' work wasn't) you never knew what you'd be doing on any given day, and you could never get on a roll in which a certain kind of investigation was followed by another of a similar kind. No, the work *they* did was always a kind of crapshoot − unpredictable, risky, or problematical − and although Jupiter would have liked to believe that The Three Investigators' recent triumphs in discovering ancient artifacts and recovering stolen treasure could be repeated in the future, he knew there was no certainty of any such thing.

No, whatever investigation might result from Ivan Fedorov being accused of plagiarism, it was impossible to imagine it would lead to anything even half as exciting as the cases in the Napa Valley and Santa Barbara. Even so, Jupiter thought, since he had given his word to Mrs. Vasiliev that The Three Investigators would tackle the matter, he thought it was time to go find Mallory, so that they could start looking into Ivan Fedorov's background.

2

A Family Of Fedorovs

Mallory had gotten to the Salvage Yard early that morning and although she, too, felt a little let down by The Three Investigators' sudden arrival back in reality-land, and she, too, missed the excitement — and even glory! — of their last two cases, she'd been looking forward to putting in a solid day's work. When school had ended for the summer, she'd expected to be spending a good part of every week right here, sorting through the various items that Uncle Titus had brought back from one of his buying expeditions. But her adventures with Jupiter, Pete, and Bob had interrupted all that — and she couldn't help but be glad of it.

Although it had turned out that Mallory was very good at sorting objects; keeping a running inventory of everything the Salvage Yard had to offer; writing pithy and clever descriptions of the individual items; then photographing them, and putting them on the Salvage Yard's website — and she got a lot of satisfaction from doing all of it — she got even more satisfaction from being part of a team that made a real difference in the world.

She was constantly surprised by the difference that team actually made – and also by how much she liked being the only girl on a team of boys. She had always liked boys better than girls – but she'd never imagined she would find three boys she liked as much as she liked The Three Investigators, both individually and together.

The previous summer, she'd had to hold herself back from what had seemed a very natural instinct to try to convince the team – Jupiter especially – that she had skills and talents that could be useful, but her holding-back had paid off in the end when Jupiter had asked her to become a Special Consultant. And then, in the very first case of the current summer, Jupiter had asked her to design a new Three Investigators headquarters.

Their old familiar meeting place had gotten crowded and cluttered – and too small for them, as they grew up! She hadn't yet started on the design, but she was hoping to do so any time now, and as she looked around her at the shed she was working in – her favorite shed, which was seeming more and more like a home away from home – she wondered if maybe she could design something a little like this.

It was quite comfortable – bright and spacious, with a sink and small refrigerator, and a seating area with an old sofa and chairs – and today she'd left the doors and windows open for maximum air.

Still, the only solid ideas she'd had so far were that maybe the new Headquarters could be called HQ2, with the old mobile home trailer called HQ1, and maybe it could have two entrances – one facing the outdoor workshop and one – smaller and more formal – facing the main gates. The side door would be a double door, making it easy to get things in and out of the (still entirely imaginary) building.

When she heard footsteps, she looked up to see Jupiter approaching. He paused in the open doorway, surrounded by sunlight. Every time she saw him unexpectedly, she found herself a bit taken aback. Of course, by now, he was as familiar to her as if he'd been a member of her family, but she was still constantly surprised by his gravity and self-possession.

He was taller now – almost as tall as Pete – and he seemed to grow leaner every week. He wore his usual outfit – a thin long-sleeved button-down cotton shirt, with the sleeves rolled up, and a pair of khaki pants –

and they hung easily on his frame, showing him to good advantage.

"Hey, Jupiter," she said. "What's up?"

"I was just talking to Aunt Mathilda, and she doesn't want me to disturb your work," he said. "I told her I wouldn't, but I find I can't help it."

"That's **OK**," Mallory said. "Come on in."

"Maybe you'd better sign out for a while. It looks like we may have a new case, and I wondered if you could do a bit of research," Jupiter said.

Without asking any questions, Mallory got to her feet and strode to the wall. She kept her time sheet on a clipboard hanging there – letting Mathilda Jones know when she started work and when she stopped. She signed out, put the clipboard back on its hook, and re-joined Jupiter.

"Let's go sit over there," she said, gesturing toward the sofa and chairs. "I'm thirsty. How about a seltzer water?"

"That sounds good," said Jupiter. "I'm just back from a bike ride to Miles Hardware."

Mallory couldn't have been happier to have Jupiter show up with a new case at the very moment when she'd been thinking about his request that she design a new Headquarters. She grabbed her laptop and put it on the battered old fruit crate she used as a coffee table, then went to get the cans of carbonated water. She and Jupiter popped the tops and drank a little before either of them spoke. She settled deeper into the sofa and put her feet up next to her computer.

"So what is it?" she asked.

Jupiter paused to gather his thoughts. "I met an older woman this morning when I was at Miles Hardware. A Russian émigré by the name of Annika Vasiliev. She has a young friend named Ivan Fedorov who's being threatened with a lawsuit. It seems some guy is alleging that Ivan, who's a singer/songwriter, stole a song from him. Mrs. Vasiliev wants us to clear Ivan's name. But proving that something didn't happen is far trickier than proving that something did. Apparently Ivan comes from a well-known Russian-American family, and Mrs. Vasiliev seemed to believe that Ivan's grandfather is so famous that everyone should have heard of him. Does the name Vadim Fedorov ring a bell for you?"

Mallory thought for a minute and then shook her head. "No," she said.

"Then let's look him up," said Jupiter.

Mallory put down her can of seltzer and picked up her laptop. Jupiter came over to sit beside her on the sofa. She typed "Vadim Fedorov" into the search engine and quickly found a lengthy entry about him.

As she read it to herself, she reported to Jupiter the basics of what she was reading.

"Wow," she said. "It looks like Mrs. Vasiliev was right. We *should* have heard of him. He was a successful screenwriter whose father was an actor named Fyodor Fedorov and who won an Oscar! And Vadim's son Yuri was a well-known musician and composer."

She and Jupiter looked at one another with some amazement.

"Who should I start with?" she asked him.

"Let's start with Ivan's great-grandfather," Jupiter said. "The actor who won the Oscar."

Mallory typed "Fyodor Fedorov" into the search engine and started reading.

"It says he was a famous Russian stage actor, best known for his roles in plays by Ostrovsky and Chekhov," she reported. "He was given a medal by the last Czar of Russia for his theater work. He left Russia after the Russian Revolution and came to Hollywood in 1917. It says he was a White Russian. Do you know what that is?”

“It's a mixed drink,” Jupiter said. “But I don't think that's what it means in this case.”

Mallory quickly looked up the term. “It's the opposite of the Reds – the Bolsheviks,” she reported. “White Russians were anti-Bolshevik – people who didn't approve of the Russian Revolution. Some White Russians stayed in Russia and fought, but others fled Russia and emigrated all around the world.”

“I can see why Fyodor fled,” Jupiter said soberly. “If he'd been decorated by the Czar, he'd have been seen as an enemy of the people by the Russian revolutionaries. One thing I know about the Russian Revolution is that they ended up shooting the Czar and his wife and all of their children in a basement. They even shot one of the daughter’s dogs.”

Mallory looked at Jupiter in shock.

“They did?” she asked him. “Really?”

“Really,” he said.

Reading further in the article, Mallory discovered that when Fyodor Fedorov had fled Russia along with his wife Marinka, and the two of them had made their way to California, Fyodor had begun a whole new career in the movies.

For a moment, Mallory concentrated on what she was reading. "It says there were a lot of Russians in Hollywood in the 1920s and 30s. And not just actors. Directors and composers, too. It seems they had a lot to contend with. They had heavy Boris-and-Natasha sorts of accents, and the actors often had to take roles they didn't want. Fyodor's greatest success was playing a Bolshevik in a movie called *Dawn over Petrograd* – about the Russian revolution. He won an Oscar for Best Supporting Actor."

"That's a new level of irony," Jupiter said, "isn't it? A White Russian winning an award for playing a Red." He shook his head. "Have you heard of the movie?" he asked.

"No," Mallory said, "but that's not surprising."

"When was it made?" Jupiter asked.

"In 1937," Mallory said. "Though the film is set in 1918."

Mallory knew basically nothing about the Russian Revolution, and very little about the Soviet Union, but at the moment all Jupiter really wanted was to know about the Fedorov family. She thought they had learned enough about Fyodor Fedorov, so she turned to his only child – looking up an obituary in the paper Bob's father worked for, the Los Angeles *Sun*.

She read the obituary aloud to Jupiter.

It seemed that Fyodor and Marinka Fedorov had named their son Vadim. He'd been born in 1920, just after they'd gotten to the United States. He grew up as an American, and a child of Hollywood. Early on, he showed great talent as a writer, and he turned his skills to screenwriting. His first success came in 1939, when he was just nineteen, and he was incredibly prolific and successful for fifteen years.

In fact, he was at the height of his fame and success when, in 1954, during the beginnings of the Cold War between Russia and America, he was suddenly accused of being a Communist. He'd lost his job and his livelihood and found that no one would hire him as a screenwriter any longer.

"Good grief," Mallory said as she relayed this information to Jupiter. "How could people imagine that the only child of two White Russians could have been a Communist or a Communist sympathizer?"

"Maybe they mixed him up with the character his father won an Oscar for," Jupiter said.

"Maybe they did," Mallory said. She read on to find out that was only partly true and that what had really happened was a simple act of malice.

Someone who had it in for Vadim — someone he'd insulted, or who was jealous of his success — reported that he had seen him at a meeting of the American Communist Party.

"Wow!" Mallory said. "This is hard to believe. One accusation and the man's life was ruined. It didn't matter that his parents had fled Russia after the Revolution, or that everyone who knew him swore he was an anti-Communist. Vadim Fedorov's career as a Hollywood screenwriter was over. A U.S. Senator named Joseph McCarthy went after people in government, the universities, the press, and the film industry, and destroyed a lot of lives. It's really scary how much damage one man with too much power can do. Though I guess this Joseph McCarthy had a lot of help."

"Does it say what happened to Vadim after he was blacklisted?" Jupiter asked.

Mallory read a bit more. "Just like his father — but for different reasons — Vadim pivoted and started a whole new career," she said. "He started writing mystery novels, under the pseudonym Edison Ford. He kept writing until he died in 2000, at the age of 80. Apparently Vadim — a.k.a. Edison Ford — was so successful as a novelist that he became quite rich — and also very reluctant to talk about the blacklisting or his life before it."

Mallory was about to read more when she heard a telephone ringing.

It was somewhat distant, but the noise carried on the morning breeze, and she knew instantly where it came from. "Headquarters!" she said, and both she and Jupiter were on their feet.

Ever since the summer before, when someone had broken in, Jupiter had stopped locking Headquarters. The two of them dashed across the gravel of the Salvage Yard and through The Three Investigators' outdoor workshop. Jupiter flung open the old door named Easy Three, and Mallory and he managed to get into Headquarters by the ninth ring — just in time.

Jupiter grabbed the base and punched speakerphone. "Hello," he said, a bit breathlessly. "This is Three Investigators Headquarters. Jupiter Jones speaking."

The voice Mallory heard was clearly a woman's but lower-pitched than most. It was accented, but easy to understand, and it conveyed a sense of authority and firmness.

"Hello, Jupiter," she said. "This is Annika Vasiliev. We met this morning?”

“Yes, Mrs. Vasiliev,” Jupiter said. “I remember you.”

“Most people do,” Mrs. Vasiliev said. “I have spoken to Ivan, and he and Cassandra will be coming to my apartment tomorrow to talk to The Three Investigators and their friend Mallory MacLeod.” She seemed quite certain that this would all work out.

Mallory smiled at Jupiter, impressed that he had mentioned her to Mrs. Vasiliev, and even more impressed that the old woman had remembered her full name.

“Ivan and Cassandra will be here in the early afternoon, after lunch,” she went on. “About 2 o'clock? Will that suit you?”

“Certainly,” Jupiter said. “The four of us will be there. We're looking forward to it. We'll see you then.”

When he hung up, he said, “I wasn't sure she’d call, but I’m glad she did. We can take our bikes. Let me get the address.”

He pulled out his wallet and took from it the scrap of paper Mrs. Vasiliev had given him and handed it to Mallory.

“She lives in the Northumberland House,” Mallory said, delighted. When Jupiter looked puzzled, she said, “It's another old Victorian. It's been divided up into apartments, like the Wessex House where I live. It's just around the corner from me."

"I thought I knew where it was," Jupiter said, "but I had no idea it was so close to you."

Mallory found herself suddenly looking forward to meeting Mrs. Vasiliev and this Ivan Fedorov. The old woman undoubtedly lived in an apartment very much like the one that Mallory shared with her mother, and in the same part of Rocky Beach. She could see Mrs. Vasiliev in her living room with the bay windows and the hanging plants and the rich old carpet on the floor, and she was flooded with a fellow feeling for the woman.

It was funny how that worked, she thought. Of course she knew that everyone had lots of things in common with everyone else. But it was always nice to find out that you shared something special and unusual, like this.

"Now that the appointment has been set," Jupiter said, "we'd better call Pete and Bob and let them know."

He was just about to pick up the receiver and start dialing when the phone rang again – so unexpectedly it made both Mallory and Jupiter jump. Jupiter looked at Mallory.

"I hope it's not Mrs. Vasiliev calling to

change the plan," Jupiter said.

He punched speakerphone again. "Three Investigators Headquarters, Jupiter Jones speaking."

This time the voice was familiar – rich and deep, full of round vowels. A speech-coached voice, and one that was familiar to moviegoers all over the world.

"Jupiter! It's Daman Duwalia," he said.

Mallory was amazed. She'd just been talking with her friend Califia not long before, and they'd mentioned that they hadn't heard from Daman in a while. Daman was in his late teens, and already a big movie star. The previous summer he'd starred in a Rocky Beach Summer Theatre production of *Romeo and Juliet*, opposite Califia. There'd been trouble on the set, which had resulted in one of The Three Investigators' more complex cases.

"Well," Jupiter said. "This *is* a surprise."

"A good one, I hope," Daman said. "Last summer, after you figured out what was going on at the theater, I promised to invite you to the premiere of whichever of my movies opened next. As it turns out, that's the latest *Time Twist*."

"*Time Twist?*" Jupiter said, as if he couldn't quite remember what that was.

"The studio is opening the film on the 4th of July," Daman said. "Next week. Afterwards, there's going to be a party at the producer's house. A barbecue, lots of food. There's a swimming pool if you're so inclined. And fireworks after it gets dark. I hope you all can come."

"It sounds terrific," Jupiter said, as cheerfully as he could manage.

Mallory laughed. From the look on Jupiter's face, she thought he'd rather walk on hot coals. He disliked all parties, and this one seemed like it might be particularly hard for him to get enthused about.

"Is that you, Mallory?" Daman said. "I thought I recognized your laugh."

"Hi, Daman," Mallory said. "It'll be good to see you again."

"It seems like an odd time to have a movie premiere," Jupiter said. "On the 4th of July."

"It won't seem odd when you see the movie," Daman said. "The whole title is *Time Twist: Independence Day*. In the movie, my character – from the future – travels back in time to the very first 4th of July – the day the Continental Congress declares the country's independence from Great Britain. It's a bit of a stretch, but it's kind of cool."

"I can't wait to see it," Jupiter said, rolling his eyes at Mallory.

"If you all can come, I'll send a limousine to pick you up. Would you please also ask Califia for me?"

"Sure," Jupiter said. "We'll be happy to."

"Califia will be so happy, Daman," Mallory said. Happy wouldn't describe it, Mallory thought. Califia would be over the moon – and so would Pete.

"Thank you very much, Daman," Jupiter said. "We'll see you next week." He hung up and looked at Mallory. "Well," he said. "Maybe it'll be fun."

"I'm sure it will be," Mallory said. "For some of us."

"My aunt and uncle and I usually go to the city park for the fireworks," Jupiter said. "But last year Bob and Pete and I were up in Jackson."

"I remember," Mallory said. "You invited me but my mother had already promised the guy she was dating that I'd go with her to some cookout. It wasn't much fun."

"I hope your mother doesn't have plans for you this year," Jupiter said. "I'd like it if you could be there at this party."

"I will be," Mallory said. "My mother's learned better. Recently, she's butted out of my life almost completely. I've convinced her I can take care of myself."

"I'm sure you can," Jupiter said. "Still, I'm a little worried."

"What about?" Mallory asked.

"About Pete," Jupiter said. He shook his head and looked grave. "I'm afraid that when he hears the news about Daman's party, he might just blow a gasket."

This time Mallory did more than smile. She laughed hard and long – because she knew that Jupiter was right. After that, she told him she thought she'd better get back to work – though when she got back to the shed she'd been working in, she actually didn't sign in again at once.

Instead, she did some additional research about what had happened to Ivan Fedorov's grandfather, Vadim. The more she read, the more disturbed she felt. She had thought it was sickening when Jupiter had told her about the czar and his family being shot in a basement after the Russian Revolution, and although the story of what happened to Vadim wasn't the same, in its own way it was sickening, too.

Still, she also found it fascinating, since after his first career was stolen from him, Vadim had just started a second one. And the pseudonym he chose to publish his detective novels under − Edison Ford − seemed like a secret message. Though Mallory couldn't be sure, it looked like he had taken the names of two of America's most iconic inventors − Thomas Edison and Henry Ford − and come up with a new persona as a way of saying he still believed in the promise of America − a place where you could reinvent yourself if you worked hard and were good at what you did.

Although he must have been enraged at being denied a job as a screenwriter and also at being falsely tarred as a Communist, Mallory thought, he had given a clue as to what he believed this country was really about. And he had been a huge success − even more of a success as a mystery writer than he'd been as a screenwriter, Mallory thought.

His novels had swum against the modern tide of violence and gore and were known for their vivid physical settings and the way the personality of the murderer blended seamlessly with the milieu in which he lived. Ford was also known for giving his readers the sense that all mysteries could be solved with a little time and care. Though being blacklisted would be enough to sour most people, Mallory thought, Edison Ford had somehow managed to rise above it – though one writer Mallory found online thought it was a pity he hadn't turned his talents to what it had actually been like.

A scholar who had studied all of his screenplays and all of his novels had written the following sentences about his work: "In another time and place, Vadim Fedorov might have been either a Catholic poet or a muckraking journalist – a man with an Ockham's Razor-like mind, a virtuous pen, and indefatigable ink. What a pity his deep well of humanity was tarnished by a savage mob."

While Mallory had no idea if the man actually deserved this praise – and wasn't entirely sure what some of it even meant – she thought it nice that he had gotten it, and she looked forward to finding out more about him the following day at Annika Vasiliev's house. Although she assumed this case wouldn't be as exciting as a case about the discovery of priceless medieval artifacts or the recovery of an ancient treasure, she had the feeling it might contain surprises, and she liked the idea that Vadim Fedorov's writing might be called "indefatigable ink."

3

At Northumberland House

Ever since Pete had learned that he, Bob, Jupiter, and Mallory – and Califia Garcia-Williams! – had been invited to the premiere of *Time Twist: Independence Day,* he'd been trying to put Daman's invitation into reasonable perspective. It wasn't as if The Three Investigators and Califia were the *only* people Daman had invited to the premiere and the party afterwards – were they? Undoubtedly a lot of other people would be there, too. Even so, as he, Bob, and Jupiter headed for the Wessex House on their bikes, Pete was having a bit of trouble concentrating on Jupiter's instructions.

"Now listen closely, both of you," Jupiter said, as the three of them pedaled.

"Our client's name is Ivan Fedorov. He's a musician who comes from a very interesting family of artists. So far, we have no reason to think that his family background has anything to do with the case we're supposed to investigate, but even so, I think I should fill the two of you in."

He went on to tell them, at some length,

what he and Mallory had discovered the day before. Though Pete was generally interested in the history, what struck him most forcefully was one small part of it.

"Wait a minute," he said. "The old guy, the great-grandfather, the one who came from Russia – "

"Fyodor Fedorov," Jupiter said.

"He and his wife had one son, and that son had one son, and that son *also* had one son?"

"That's correct," Jupiter said. "Each of three generations had a single male child."

"Whoa!" Pete said.

"That's not *so* odd," Bob said. "I mean, look at the three of us. All our parents only had one kid, and we're all boys."

"Well, if you put it that way," Pete said. "But for three generations? I may be an only child, but it's pretty unusual in my family. I have loads of aunts and uncles, and they all had kids, so I have tons of cousins."

"Is this your father's side of the family you're talking about?" Bob asked.

"Yes," Pete said. "My mother has a sister, and she has three kids, but it's my dad who has *lots* of brothers and sisters."

Just then, they arrived on Mallory's

street. Mallory was on the front porch waving, and as Pete cheerfully waved back, he thought her red hair looked particularly fiery against the pale green paint of the Wessex House.

"You guys hot?" she asked. "Do you want something to drink?'

"Thank you," Jupiter said, "but no. We took our time." He glanced at his watch. "I think we ought to proceed."

They parked their bikes and locked them, ditched their helmets, straightened their clothes, and followed Mallory around the corner to the Northumberland House.

A silver van with sliding side doors and a sunroof was parked in the driveway. It was relatively new, and Pete couldn't resist a look inside. He could tell right away that it belonged to Ivan Fedorov. It had two front bucket seats, and strands of cheap Mardi Gras beads hung from the rear view mirror. Through the back window, Pete saw a number of puffy paisley-covered cushions and two guitar amplifier cabinets next to each other.

Pete had seen ones like them in the band room at the high school. They were black rectangular boxes with silver-threaded mesh covering the front, and, in the upper left corner, large chrome script spelled the word "Fender."

Pete also saw three instrument cases – one rectangular and two guitar-shaped – that he thought must hold a keyboard and two electric guitars. There was also a case for an acoustic guitar. Although he imagined the van's contents were safe for the time being, he hoped Ivan didn't leave his stuff there overnight. Maybe he was going to play a gig later.

By this time, Jupiter had mounted the steps to the porch and was examining the names on the various ground-floor apartments. Before Pete knew it, Jupiter was knocking on a door. He hurried to join his friends. The door opened and an old woman stood there. Her gray hair had been neatly plaited and hung in a single braid over her left shoulder. She peered down at them with satisfaction.

She didn't look unfriendly, but Pete could see right away that she wasn't the warm cuddly grandmother type. She tapped on the floor with the cane she was carrying.

"You are right on time," she said. "That is a very good sign. Enter, please." She spoke with an accent Pete recognized from dastardly spies he'd seen in several espionage movies. "I am Annika Vasiliev."

She stepped aside, and Jupiter, Bob, and Mallory filed in. Pete followed them. The apartment was dim. Mrs. Vasiliev had pulled the shades halfway down against the day's glare. The room contained two overstuffed old-fashioned sofas with intricately carved wooden legs, as well as an easy chair with an ottoman.

A dark wooden sideboard stood against one wall with a large silver urn upon it, gleaming dully in the spare light. The side tables were also made of dark highly varnished wood. Intricate lace doilies had been arranged across the tops of the sofas and chair. In the shaded bay window stood a potted rubber plant and a banana tree with wilting yellow leaves. The air smelled of cinnamon or sandalwood. Pete felt as though he had walked out of California and into another country, across the sea and back in time.

He stopped staring when Jupiter introduced him, Bob, and Mallory to Mrs. Vasiliev. Her eyes glinted when she caught his.

"I am sorry it is so dark in here," she said. "The strong light hurts my eyes. Getting old is – how you say? – no picnic."

She didn't look that old to Pete, and she had enough energy for someone much younger. "Come," she said. "I will introduce you."

A young man and young woman hovered at the far edge of the room, looking at them expectantly. "Ivan, Cassandra," Mrs. Vasiliev said. "These are the young people I told you about."

The man stepped forward and nodded at the four of them. "I'm Ivan Fedorov," he said. "I'm pleased to meet you."

The first thing Pete noticed was how ordinary Ivan looked. He wasn't handsome or sexy, the way a movie star like Daman Duwalia would have been. His features were unremarkable. He had a wide forehead and his brownish-blond hair, cut relatively short, fell across it. His eyes were gray and his nose a bit broad. When he smiled, his eyes crinkled. He also looked very young – especially for someone who had written a song for a Hollywood movie.

Before Pete could say anything, Ivan put his arm around the young woman and drew her forward. "This is my wife Cassandra Abelman," he said.

Cassandra smiled shyly and nodded. She was very pretty, Pete thought, but she certainly was not doing anything to call attention to that fact. She wore no makeup, and her clothes were as plain as could be – a pair of nondescript jeans and a blue chambray shirt. But her hair was incredible. Reddish-blond and long and naturally curly, it cascaded in corkscrew curls over her shoulders.

Though he now noticed that there were wedding rings on their fingers, Pete was amazed that these two were actually married. He couldn't help but blurt out, "How old are you two, anyway?"

Ivan laughed. "We're twenty-three," he said, "though I've always looked younger than my age. A blessing or a curse, depending. But I know how old the four of you are. Annika said you were all fourteen. Her friend who owns the hardware store in Rocky Beach told her."

"Almost fifteen," Pete said defensively. "And we're real investigators, really."

That seemed to be the signal for Jupiter to whip out his wallet. Now he handed the firm's business card to Ivan, who looked at it carefully, then put it away in the pocket of his shirt.

"Thank you for this," he said. "Annika already showed me the one you gave to her."

"Come," Mrs. Vasiliev said. "We cannot talk like this." She ushered them all into the room where they took seats on the two sofas. Pete found himself sitting next to Cassandra and Ivan, while Jupiter, Bob, and Mallory sat on the other sofa.

"You must help yourselves," Mrs. Vasiliev said, putting a silver dish with salted nuts down on the dark coffee table next to another dish filled with cubes of sugar. "We will have tea."

It was summer and Pete was expecting iced tea, so he was surprised when Mrs. Vasiliev went to the sideboard and began filling small glass cups in silver holders with piping hot tea from the urn there.

"Did you bring the samovar from Russia?" Mallory asked.

Mrs. Vasiliev looked keenly at the girl. "No, my dear," she said. "We could bring almost nothing when we came. I found this many years ago at the wonderful salvage yard of Jupiter's aunt and uncle. When I met him I wasn't aware that he was related to the Salvage Yard – but that, too, I was told by Miles Szabó. The samovar is much like the one I had in Moscow." She looked triumphant.

"Wow!" Pete said. "That's amazing!" Even Jupiter seemed impressed and pleased by the coincidence.

Pete was surprised at how dark the tea in the cup was – black tea. He looked around for milk but there was none on offer. Mrs. Vasiliev caught him looking. "Young man," she said. "We will drink like we did in Russia. Let me show you." She took a sugar cube from the dish and placed it between her teeth. Then she carefully sipped her tea through it.

Pete was fascinated. He tried to follow her example, but he found the sugar cube collapsing in his mouth and the tea scalded his tongue.

"No, no," Mrs. Vasiliev said from the easy chair. "Just the tiny sip. You must try again."

O.K., Pete thought. But I'll take a break first.

He looked across at his friends – who were being a good deal more cautious than he had been. Then he took another look at Ivan Fedorov. From this angle, he could see what an open and appealing face the young man had, even if he wasn't strikingly handsome. He looked smart and genuinely interested in others. Pete was also struck by how close Ivan and Cassandra seemed. They looked at one another frequently, smiling, and one of them was constantly reaching out to touch the other's arm or knee.

The strangeness of drinking tea in this

fashion seemed to shut everyone up, so Pete decided to take it upon himself to get the conversation going.

He turned to Cassandra. "Are you a musician too?" he asked. "I peeked in your van and you have a lot of instruments!"

Cassandra laughed. "No," she said. "All those instruments are Ivan's. He plays electric and acoustic guitar and piano and trumpet, and he also composes music. I'm a writer – a poet, really. Of course Ivan's a poet too." She reached out unconsciously and touched his knee again. "His lyrics are poems, in my opinion, and his songs are just poems set to music."

"That's how we got together," Ivan said. "Cassandra liked my music and I liked her poetry. And then we found out we both loved the work of the same other people."

"Like who?" Mallory asked.

"Oh," Cassandra said. "I don't know. Lots of people. Like Leonard Cohen. He was an Ashkenazi Jew, like me – and also like Asher Cohen, the computer whiz who founded Freedom Digital. He went to the same temple I did when I was growing up in Boxwood. I don't know why I mentioned that, actually – since he's no relation to Leonard Cohen!"

"I've heard of him, though," Bob said.

He's a billionaire, isn't he? The founder of Freedom Digital?"

"I think so," said Cassandra. "At least he owns a big estate in the San Jacinto Mountains. Anyway, your question was about artists who both Ivan and I love. Leonard Cohen was Canadian – born in Toronto – but he spent some time in a Buddhist monastery right here in Los Angeles."

"Jupiter was born in Toronto too!" Pete said.

"Really?" Ivan said. "When did you move to the United States?"

"My parents were killed in a car crash when I was an infant," Jupiter said in the neutral voice he always used to talk about his life. "I was brought to California to live with my aunt and uncle and I've been here ever since. As Mrs. Vasiliev mentioned, they own a salvage yard here in Rocky Beach."

Mrs. Vasiliev nodded emphatically.

"I'm sorry about your parents," Ivan said. He looked very thoughtful. "Death is a very big deal, don't you think? So final and sometimes so sudden. My father died, two years ago, when I was 21, and I'm still not over the shock. He was only sixty-seven years old. He had lung cancer – from smoking – and he died just four months after the doctors told him. I was shocked by how quickly it happened, and also by how much I missed him."

"Gee," Pete said. "That's too bad. I'm sorry. What did your father do?" He thought Jupiter had told him, but right now he couldn't remember.

"He was a musician, like me," Ivan said. "Actually he was more of a composer than a performer. He worked in the movie business like his grandfather and father. He wrote soundtracks. His name was Yuri Fedorov, and the trouble I'm in could actually be connected to him. This guy Colton Clark who's threatening me with a lawsuit? My father was instrumental in getting him fired from a movie."

"So you think he may be trying to get revenge on you for something your father did?" Jupiter asked.

"It's possible," Ivan said. "Colton and I went to high school together in L.A., and though we weren't friends, I thought we were friendly. We both played in the marching band and the orchestra, and sometimes we jammed together at parties."

"Can you tell us any more about Colton?" Jupiter asked.

"He's got some talent," Ivan said, "to be

fair. But he's squandered it so far. He parties all the time and he's into drinking and drugs. He's done a lot of stupid stuff and was even arrested once, but his father got him off.

"Anyway, Colton was hired to play the role of a band member in a film that my father wrote the soundtrack for, and when he showed up drunk one time too often, my father got seriously angry. He complained to the director, who fired Colton. The band's music in the movie got all sorts of notice and the other band members went on to some fantastic gigs. But not Colton. He was really bitter."

"And now that Ivan's career is about to take off," Cassandra said, "here he comes with this threat of a lawsuit."

"I wrote this song and did a bunch of the instrumentals for this movie about Catherine the Great – "

"It's an amazing song," Cassandra said fervently.

" – and Colton's claiming that I stole the melody and words from him," Ivan said. "He swears we went to the same high school graduation party, and that we jammed together, and that he wrote this song I later supposedly stole. It's true I was at the party, but we didn't play together that night, and besides,

I left way early and went home. I was dating Cassandra the whole time I was writing the song, and she knows how it changed and changed until it reached its final form."

Ivan shook his head in bewilderment that something like this could be happening to him.

"We don't see how Colton could actually win this," Cassandra said. "But Ivan's lawyer said the whole thing could take years to grind its way through the courts, and Ivan's name would be under a cloud all that time, and the worst thing is that the director is threatening to scrap the song from the movie because he doesn't want any bad publicity."

"What would he do for the music if he did that?" Pete asked.

"He'd just hire someone else to write a different song," Ivan said. "He loves what I wrote, but he's more concerned with his own career than with mine. He's afraid that Colton's lawyer might even get an injunction to prevent the release of the film."

"Have you tried sitting down and talking to this guy?" Mallory asked.

"It's impossible," Ivan said. "He just keeps lying, and he's nasty and condescending, and he keeps talking about how his father could really hurt me if he wanted to."

Cassandra sat forward eagerly and swept her gaze from Pete to Jupiter to Mallory to Bob.

"That's why we thought the four of you might be able to help. When Annika told us you were investigators, we thought maybe you could track down some of the other people who were at that graduation party and could corroborate Ivan's side of the story – that he left early and didn't really jam with Colton Clark. Because you're young and not very threatening – I mean, you're high school students, not police officers or private investigators or lawyers – maybe they'll open up to you in a way they just wouldn't with adults with more authority."

That idea made sense to Pete, but compared to their last two, this didn't seem like a very thrilling case so far. About a two on the Excito-meter. Still, he found that he really liked Ivan and Cassandra and Mrs. Vasiliev, and was sorry for Ivan's troubles.

Even Jupiter looked a little glum about the way things were shaping up. "Is there any way you can think of for the four of us to meet Colton Clark?" he asked. "Without letting him know we're trying to help you, Ivan?"

Ivan shook his head in puzzlement, but Cassandra spoke. "You could meet him at my book party," she said. "I'm pretty sure he's coming with his older sister Tracey. She's a member of my writing group, and I invited the whole group before the threats about the lawsuit started happening."

"That's right!" Ivan said. "Cassandra's first book of poems!" He looked at her fondly.

"What's a book party?" Pete asked.

Cassandra looked bashful. "Just a group of people getting together to celebrate the publication of a new book," she said. "Mine's called *The House I Lived In*, and it's being put out by a small press called Pacific View. They're doing a really good job with publicity. Other publishers and book review editors and people in the book business will be there, along with people I've invited. The thing is, Tracey Clark is actually the one who introduced me to the editor who's publishing the book, so I can't really disinvite her – even if she *is* bringing her wretched brother."

"It's tomorrow afternoon at Books & Bistro down in Los Angeles," Ivan said. "I don't know why I didn't think of it. You could all come!"

"Do you and Tracey get along?" Mallory said. "What's your writing group like?"

"We get along fine," Cassandra said,

"though we're not really friends. The whole writing group thing is kind of weird, if you want to know the truth. We meet every couple of weeks at someone's house and a few of us read recent work we've written and then everyone talks about it. It's supposed to be about constructive criticism, but mainly it's a support group. Seven women and three men. Most of them write fiction. I'm the only poet, so it's not much use to me as a writer. Hardly any, really. I go mostly for the camaraderie. Writing can be lonely sometimes."

"It wouldn't be strange if we all showed up?" Bob asked.

"Not at all," Cassandra said. "The party was advertised, so it's more or less open to the public. Pacific View took out an ad in the L.A. *Sun*. Books & Bistro is on the corner of Encinitas and Olvera. It starts at 5:00 and should be over by 7:00. If you come, we can all go back to our house afterwards to draw up a plan. We'll order pizza!"

"But if we talk to this Colton Clark, won't he be suspicious?" Pete asked.

"We can't go as The Three Investigators, obviously," Mallory said, "and we can't be there to be talking only to him. At least not in our cover story."

"Cover story?" Mrs. Vasiliev asked with interest.

"Our reason for being there," Mallory said. "I think we should keep it as close to the truth as possible. Maybe we should be high school students who've been assigned a joint summer paper on the media business in southern California – publishing, music, movies, that sort of thing. We could tell anyone who asks that we're taking a course called Media in America in the fall. We saw the ad in the paper and wrote to Cassandra, asking if we could come to the party to do research."

Pete was impressed. Mallory was really good at this pretending-to-be-someone-else thing.

Ivan and Cassandra were impressed too. "That's a great idea," Ivan said. "A party like that would be a good place to find out stuff about the media business. Though I don't know what Colton Clark could tell you."

"That doesn't matter," Mallory said. "It's just a way in."

"It would be even better," Jupiter said, "if we could use this supposed collaborative paper as an ongoing reason to hang out with the two of you, if necessary."

"That's no problem," Ivan said. "After

all, I *am* a musician and Cassandra *is* a writer, and if the subject ever came up with Tracey or Colton, we could just say we invited you to hang around with us for the next few days."

"Here's another thought," Cassandra said. "What if the focus of your paper wasn't the media business itself but the Fedorov family – four generations of Russian-Americans, all of whom have been successful in one or another aspect of the American media – starting with Ivan's great-grandfather Fyodor, who was an actor in the early days of Hollywood."

"That's a great idea," Mallory said.

"Actually," Cassandra went on, "Ivan and I met because of his great-grandfather. My father's a film historian who works at the American Film History Library."

"I know where that is," Bob said. "It's in Boxwood, about twenty minutes from Rocky Beach. My father took me there once."

"My father's writing a book about Russian émigrés who left Russia after the Revolution and made their way to southern California during what he calls the Golden Age of Hollywood," Cassandra said. "It centers on Fyodor Fedorov and other actors, but also includes composers and directors. As part of his research, my father interviewed Yuri Fedorov,

66

Ivan's father."

"Wow!" Bob said. "That's really interesting. I'm a bit of a history nut − not the history of film in particular, just history in general. My father loves history, too."

Mrs. Vasiliev got up from her easy chair. She had been listening carefully to the conversation, nodding from time to time. When Ivan and Cassandra had been talking about Colton Clark, she looked as though the room had been invaded by a particularly noxious smell.

"All of this is very good," she said. "Very good. Too many young people these days are frivolous. But The Three Investigators have a plan!"

"Yes," Jupiter said. "We have a plan. Will you be at the book party, Mrs. Vasiliev?"

"Me?" Mrs. Vasiliev said. "No, no. That is for you young people. Cassandra invited me, which was very kind. She knows I congratulate her with all my heart, but I can talk to her whenever I want to in my own house. I do not need to stand around at some bookstore."

"But with pizza afterwards!" Pete said cheerfully.

"And a big debriefing," Bob said as they all got up and headed for the door.

"Oh, Ivan," Pete said, turning back. "I almost forgot."

"Yes?" Ivan said.

"You don't leave all your instruments in the back of your van overnight, do you?"

Ivan laughed. "No," he said. "Don't worry, Pete. They're always safe inside my house."

"Good!" Pete said. "That's a relief."

"We can count on Pete," Bob said. "He takes care of all the little details." He looked playfully at Pete as Jupiter and Mallory snorted.

"What?" Pete asked. "What's so funny?" He actually felt a little hurt at being teased by his friends for having taken the time to warn Ivan. The thing was, he'd been far more taken with both Ivan and Cassandra than he'd expected to be. In fact, he suddenly saw them as some pretty unusual role models for a guy like him – a guy who was hoping to get a girlfriend soon. And not just any girlfriend, but one who was a sort of artist, too!

4

A Tale Cut Short By A Tail

The next afternoon, Bob sat in the back yard of his house, on the patio off the kitchen, thinking about the Fedorovs. He'd spent a hectic morning working at the library – shelving books, helping patrons, and soothing Miss Bennett's nerves about the newsletter, which he edited. The fact was, right at the moment, he was wishing someone would soothe *his* nerves. That morning his father had told Bob that he'd had to fight like hell to convince his editor not to publish an out and out hit piece on The Three Investigators in the Los Angeles *Sun*.

The piece had been written by a female opinion columnist who also happened to be a part-time mystery writer and who had argued in her piece that there was simply no way on earth that The Three Investigators could possibly have solved all the cases they had claimed to. She'd also taken issue with the way Bob had written the cases up – and said outright that it seemed to her outlandish that the Coast Guard had responded to an SOS from a lighthouse on private property.

Of course, that was exactly what had happened, but the opinion columnist hadn't been worried about *that*. Proving her argument with facts had been a time-consuming task she couldn't be bothered with, and although Bob was happy his father's editor had been convinced that what she'd written was straight-out slander, it had still left him shaken to learn that someone he had never met – and to whom he'd done nothing – had sat down at her desk to try and hurt him and his friends.

What made it even worse was that Bob's father had told him that his own job was getting harder all the time – that journalism in general was getting corrupted. There was less and less concern in the newsrooms and the editorial boards about the story itself, and more and more emphasis on whether it was told by someone with the right credentials and the approved point of view. The right credentials, as a concept, were always shifting, and Bob's father was wondering just how long he could go on working for the *Sun*.

A few months ago, he'd started working on a book about education in America, and he was thinking that if he made a success at that, he might resign from his job. Right now, however, his father was at the paper, his mother was at her lab at Reedmore College, and he himself was trying to do some research before The Three Investigators got in the car with Worthington and took off for Cassandra Abelman's book reception.

In addition to everything else, Bob was a bit apprehensive about *that*. He was a terrible actor – unlike Jupiter and Mallory who were quite expert. Bob stuttered and hemmed and hawed and blushed when he was asked to be someone other than himself. He remembered his abject failure in The Three Investigators' last case, when he had tried to pretend he hadn't noticed a piece of incriminating evidence when he actually had, and later today he'd be asked to pretend that he was working on a collaborative paper for his upcoming Media in America class, when there was no paper and no such class.

The very idea of it made him squirm. He could still be himself, Bob Andrews, which was a good thing, but he thought he had better bone up on Ivan Fedorov's family before anyone started asking him questions. The person he found himself most interested in was Vadim Fedorov, Ivan's grandfather – a writer who'd started out by writing screenplays and ended up writing detective stories.

Ever since Bob had started writing up The Three Investigators cases and posting them online, he'd been thinking, privately, that maybe he'd end up as a writer himself when he grew up – though what kind of writer he wasn't certain. For a while, mainstream journalist had been at the top of the list, but with the recent news from his father, he thought he'd better push it down to the bottom for a while.

Still, even before his father had told him about the opinion piece he'd managed to get quashed, Bob had been thinking about maybe someday turning his talents to fiction. He had recently found a collection of fantasies that had originally been published in the 1940s, and one of them – a story called "The Book and The Beast" – had really taken his fancy.

In it, Waldo Dexter – a passionate collector of books and manuscripts devoted to magic and witchcraft – had discovered, in a small secondhand store, a volume bound in leather of an unusual purplish-black, and when he'd managed to open the lock on the iron band holding it closed, he'd seen that the book was handwritten in ink, with flowing letters so ornate as to be almost unreadable.

At the top of the first page, in the bold, flowing script, was written in Italian: *Recipes and*

Conjurations, and as he flipped through the pages of the volume, Waldo Dexter saw tantalizing headings like *To Be Invisible* and *To Make A Demon Bring Three Bags Of Gold.*

Still, what made the story wonderful was how playful and funny it was – the way in which the writer assumed that his readers would enjoy the same kind of story *he* did, and would therefore be attentive to the delightfully punchy clues with which he studded his tale. The story was set in New York City, and because Waldo Dexter failed to pay proper attention to a bit of what he considered doggerel on the first page – verse he finally translated as: *Ope not this book/Twixt dusk and dawn/Lest you let loose/The devil's spawn* – the New York City police department ended up with a missing person's case.

Even the end of the story was funny.

"Except for one small point, the authorities in the end were able to explain the whole affair rather neatly.

"The bones, they concluded, represented the victims of McKenzie Muir, a homicidal maniac who lured people to his residence, killed them, and buried them in the cellar. Undoubtedly he had so treated his unfortunate friend, Waldo Dexter. Then Muir, becoming frightened, had cleverly vanished.

"Later he had returned to the locked house to burn it and destroy the evidence of his crimes, and himself had perished in the flames — for, easily recognizable among the grisly relics dug forth by the searchers, had been McKenzie Muir's dentures.

"Thus almost all the loose ends were cleverly tied up. The only point for which the authorities never were able to offer any plausible explanation was the question of what, exactly, a sabre-tooth tiger was doing in the house."

Now, *that*, Bob considered, was *writing!* The way the writer of the story had tied up his *own* loose ends by making fun of the way the rather unimaginative and even dim-witted authorities had failed to allow for the sudden appearance of ancient spells and actual *magic* in their investigation — it had made Bob laugh aloud.

Oh, well, Bob thought, enough about *that* for now. It really *was* time to do some research. He'd just located a long appreciative article about Vadim Fedorov's mystery novels when he heard a noise at the side gate leading into the backyard. He frowned, thinking his mother had come home early, and then he heard Mallory's voice.

"Bob?" she called. "Are you back there?"

"Hey, Mallory," he said. He ran to the gate and let her in.

She propped her bike against the fence and joined him.

"What's up?" he asked.

"I finished my work at the Salvage Yard," Mallory said, "and I was planning to spend a nice relaxing hour or two at home, but my mother was there and she was driving me crazy with questions. So I thought I'd ride over and see if you were home."

"I'm glad you did," Bob said.

Mallory pointed to his open laptop. "What are you up to?" she asked.

"Just doing research and making some notes," Bob said. "I made this chart of the Fedorov men, in order to keep them straight. It's a little tricky with all the unfamiliar names."

He showed her a document he'd made the night before.

1. Fyodor Fedorov, born in Russia, came to the U.S. Actor. (Ivan's great-grandfather)

2. Vadim Fedorov. Screenwriter and mystery writer. (Ivan's grandfather)

3. Yuri Fedorov. Composer. (Ivan's father)

4. Ivan Fedorov. Musician. Married to Cassandra.

"That's really helpful," Mallory said.

"Plus, I found this really long article about Ivan's grandfather," Bob said, "and I was just about to read it."

Mallory was studying Bob's laptop. "I've already read that article," she said. "Vadim Fedorov was really something. When his first career was stolen from him, he just started a second one."

Bob thought of telling Mallory about the slanderous opinion piece his father had just barely managed to squelch. But instead he said, "You know what I find really incredible? That someone was able to ruin Vadim Fedorov's life just by saying they had supposedly seen him once at a meeting of the American Communist Party. I thought free association was guaranteed by the Constitution."

"I know," Mallory said. "And what's even more incredible is the way this thing with Colton Clark and Ivan Fedorov mirrors what happened to Ivan's grandfather."

Bob had been thinking the exact same thing.

"I know!" he exclaimed. "The only proof

this Colton Clark has is his own word that he jammed with Ivan at that party. It's amazingly easy to say that something happened at a big gathering, with a lot of people there. How do you disprove it?"

"And I'd bet that whoever accused Vadim of being a Communist was driven by professional jealousy and envy, the same way that Colton Clark's jealousy is driving his accusations about Ivan," Mallory said.

Once again Bob thought of telling Mallory what his father had told him, but once again he didn't. He thought it might sound a little arrogant to compare something that hadn't even actually happened to him and the rest of The Three Investigators to the genuine destruction of Vadim Fedorov's career in the movies, and the threatened destruction of his grandson's.

Even so, they actually *were* pretty similar, and it wasn't hard for Bob to imagine just how unfair it must seem to any writer who was doing his best to make his readers (or his viewers or his listeners) laugh or cry or think about something that mattered to human beings, and to suddenly have someone appear out of nowhere determined to stop their communication. That was why the First Amendment was the first amendment, and not the second or third or fourth — because without it, no one could be certain they could communicate what was really in their hearts.

"I bet you're right," Bob said. "About the professional jealousy and envy. I wish I could talk to someone who actually knew Vadim. Another mystery writer, maybe."

It suddenly occurred to him that he knew at least one mystery writer himself — The Three Investigators' old friend Hector Sebastian! Hector had gotten involved with The Three Investigators early on, and for a while, when the boys were younger, he had written up their cases. He had a house in Dial Canyon, south of Rocky Beach, but he'd moved to Wyoming for a while because he wanted to set his mysteries in the Old West, and he wanted to soak up atmosphere.

"I wonder if Hector Sebastian knew Edison Ford," he suddenly said to Mallory. "I mean, he would have been young and Ford would have been old, but I get the impression that mystery writers often know one another."

"What a terrific idea!" Mallory said. "Why don't you call him and ask?"

"Maybe I will," Bob said. "It'd be good to talk to Hector anyway. You've never met him, but I'm sure you'd like him a lot. He's great."

"There's no time like the present," Mallory said.

"Now?" Bob said. Then he realized that Mallory was right – now was as good a time as any. In the past, when he'd talked to Hector, they'd used Skype, and that required advanced planning. But if all he wanted to do was ask Hector about Edison Ford, a phone call would be fine.

"He's in Wyoming," he reminded Mallory, "on a ranch in a little town called Dubois. It's an hour later there. Do you think that's a problem?"

Mallory glanced at her watch. "None at all," she said, "but if you're going to call, you should do it now. We have to get to the Salvage Yard pretty soon."

Bob dug his cellphone out of his pocket, checked Hector's number in the address book on his laptop, then dialed the number, sitting hunched over the patio table while Mallory sat back in her chair, her arms folded on her chest, her feet crossed and sticking out in front of her.

Hector Sebastian picked up on the fourth ring.

"Hello? Hello?" he said. There was

static, and his voice wavered in loudness, moving in and out. Bob thought he heard something whooshing in the background – something like wind.

"Mr. Sebastian," Bob said. "It's me. Bob Andrews."

"Whoa!" Mr. Sebastian said. "Steady, fella."

Mr. Sebastian had never talked to him like that before, and Bob was puzzled.

"Mr. Sebastian?" he said again. "It's – "

"Yes!" Mr. Sebastian said. "Bob! I'm thrilled that you called." There was that whooshing sound again, and then Mr. Sebastian's voice came in more clearly. "I'm in the saddle, Bob. I told you I wanted to learn how to ride a horse. Can you imagine? At my age?"

"You're on horseback right now?" Bob asked.

"Yes, indeed," Mr. Sebastian said. "Reese Carson gave me lessons. He's the owner of the ranch where I'm renting the cabin. He didn't say I'm a natural, but so far I've stayed on the horse. I'm on my own right now, and a little tipsy."

"You've been drinking?" Bob asked.

"No, of course not," Mr. Sebastian said. "A little unsteady. Usually I hold the reins with both hands, but now I'm holding the phone, you see."

"Shall I call you back later?" Bob asked.

"No," Mr. Sebastian said. "Not at all. It's wonderful to hear from you. I've been meaning to call you. I'm flying back to California in a week or so. I have my house back for July and August and I'm looking forward to seeing the three of you. And I very much look forward to meeting this Mallory MacLeod I've read so much about."

"So you're moving back?" Bob asked.

"I think I'll stay in Wyoming for another year, but I haven't completely decided," Hector said. "Still, I have people to visit back in California. With this writing business, you have to keep in contact with people, remind them you're still alive and hungry."

"It'll be great to see you!" Bob said, "Wait 'til I tell Jupiter and Pete! Could you hold on a second?"

He put his hand over the receiver and asked Mallory if she wanted him to put the call on speakerphone. She looked intrigued and nodded.

"Everything O.K. there in Rocky Beach?" Hector Sebastian asked.

"Yes," Bob said. "I'm actually with Mallory MacLeod right now, and if it's O.K. with you, I'm going to put us on speakerphone so that she can hear what's going on."

"That's fine!" Hector Sebastian said. "Hello, Mallory!"

"Hello, Mr. Sebastian!" said Mallory.

Bob tried to picture Mr. Sebastian on a horse and was having trouble. He was short and plump and genial and usually had a pipe in his hand. Bob could ride, and he'd seen a lot of westerns, so his mind was suddenly filled with spurs and chaps and saddles and craggy-looking cowboys. Was Hector wearing a bandana? Bob wondered. A cowboy hat?

"Are you sure you don't want to hold the reins with both hands?" Bob asked. He thought that maybe these weren't the best conditions under which to have this talk.

"Not a bit of it!" Hector said enthusiastically. "I'm fine. Never been better. So what's on your mind?"

Bob decided to go for it. "The case we're working on involves a musician named Ivan Fedorov," he said. "I suddenly wondered if you might have met his grandfather, Vadim Fedorov. You'd have known him by his pen name, Edison Ford. He wrote mysteries, too."

"Steady, Pepper!" Hector Sebastian

said. "Easy, fella."

"Mr. Sebastian?" Bob said.

"Yes, Bob," Hector Sebastian said. "I'm here. What a strange and wonderful question! As a matter of fact, I *did* know Edison Ford. Not well, of course. He was much, much older than I am. He must have been 70 and I was in my early 20s when I met him. I'd only just gotten started as a mystery writer, and I was attending a meeting of the Southern California branch of the MWA."

"The what?" Bob asked.

"The Southern California branch of the Mystery Writers of America," Mr. Sebastian said. "He was sitting in an easy chair, a bit apart. Everyone referred to him as Edison. I was in awe of him, and I wasn't the only one. He'd written twenty-five or thirty books by then, and had won a whole shelf of Edgars."

"What's an Edgar?" Bob asked.

"It's a painted plaster bust of Edgar Allen Poe," Mr. Sebastian said, "about eight inches high. He has black slick-backed hair and a funny downturned mustache, and he's wearing a stiff-necked white shirt, a purple vest, and a black cravat. It's a silly little thing, but it's the most prestigious award in the mystery genre. Everyone who wins one is very proud, and deservedly so. They're hard to get."

"Have you won one?" Bob asked, curious.

"Not yet," Hector Sebastian said cheerfully. "But I keep hoping! Anyway, I met Edison at that first meeting, and he couldn't have been more gracious – even to me, a young whippersnapper still wet behind the ears. Of course, my work wasn't anything like his, but we hit it off. Behind his courtliness and kindness, he seemed a little lonely. His wife had recently died, and I'm a good listener, if I do say so myself. I was flattered that he took an interest in me."

"Did you see him frequently?" Bob asked.

"Steady, Pepper," Mr. Sebastian said. "What was that? Frequently? No, no. Just at MWA functions. I used to sit with him at the awards dinners and at the local meetings. But I've always remembered one evening he and I spent together."

"Why?" Bob asked.

"One night, after a particularly boring meeting – all this ratification of by-laws and what-not – a small group of us went to a bar afterwards. We started talking about how we'd gotten interested in writing mysteries. Edison had had several drinks by then, as I remember, and he said that he'd been drawn to the mystery genre because it was one place where the writer was totally in charge, and whoever he made into a villain he could punish with impunity. In fact, he *had* to punish him. That was the way a mystery worked – what the reader expected. I thought he must be thinking of several villains he'd have liked to punish but hadn't been able to. Real life villains, of course."

"Is that the way *you* think mysteries work?" Bob asked.

"By and large," Mr. Sebastian said. "But it turned out that wasn't what Edison really wanted to talk about. He said that, in a regular novel, you didn't have that kind of formula, and things could get unpredictable, even out of control. Really, he said, you never knew from day to day what was going to happen."

"It sounds like he was speaking from experience," Bob said.

"I thought so, too!" Mr. Sebastian said. "But he said he wasn't. He said he had a friend who'd been working for almost twenty years on a novel narrated by a man when he'd suddenly realized that the narrator should be a woman. The wife of the man who'd been the narrator to begin with."

There was that whooshing sound again.

"Pepper!" Mr. Sebastian said. "Put your tail back where it belongs! You're going to knock my cellphone out of my hand!"

"That's fascinating," Bob said.

"Yes," said Mr. Sebastian. "In fact, I was so impressed that I decided, right then and there, to write a book narrated by a woman, too! It wasn't the best book I've ever written, but it wasn't the worst one, either – and, if you can believe it, my editor had the gall to tell me I would either have to change the narrator's sex or publish the book under a female pseudonym!"

"What did you do?" Mallory asked.

"I changed editors and publishers!" Mr. Sebastian said. "That was some time ago, though. I'm not sure it would be as easy nowadays to find a publishing house that would be willing to let a male writer publish a book narrated by a woman. These days, everything is about who you are, not what you can do."

In different words, this was a lot like what Bob's father had said that very morning. That these days there was less and less concern in the newsrooms and the editorial boards about the story itself, and more and more emphasis on whether or not it was told by someone with the right credentials, or the approved point of view.

Just then, Bob heard little smooching noises − air kisses or something. What was Mr. Sebastian doing?

"Are you kissing your horse?" he asked.

"Ha ha HA!" Mr. Sebastian said. "Of course not. That kissing noise tells Pepper I want him to up his gait. He's just moseying along right now, and I don't have all day. O.K., Pepper, that's fast enough. Easy now, slow."

"Everything all right, Mr. Sebastian?"

"I'm just having a little trouble here with Pepper," Hector said. "Animals are wonderful, of course, but they don't speak English and they hear things that we can't. It can be a bit disconcerting."

Bob heard a sudden intake of breath and a yell. "Mr. Sebastian?" he said.

"Whoa! Whoa!" Mr. Sebastian yelled. "Pepper! Halt! Desist! Bob, I have to go. I − "

Bob heard another yell and he pictured a cellphone in slow motion as it tumbled through the air and came to rest among rocks and dirt. The call was cut off.

He smiled. He was sure Mr. Sebastian had hung on and that Pepper would soon be gotten under control. He was glad he had called, and that before Pepper had gotten a bit too frisky, Hector had had a chance to tell his tale. A tale cut short by a tail, Bob thought, smiling to himself.

"That was great," Mallory said. "I liked that guy a lot." She looked at her watch. "We don't have much more time, but Jupiter mentioned this morning that if I could find out anything about Colton Clark before meeting him, that would be good."

"Let's do it," Bob said. Soon they were poring over articles together — though even as they did this, part of Bob's mind was considering Hector's story about the friend of Vadim Fedorov who'd worked on a book for twenty years, then had had to start the book over when he realized he was writing from the wrong point of view.

Books were really amazing, and the people who wrote them even more so, Bob thought. Well, not *all* of them, of course — but the ones you could really trust. Like the guy who'd written the story in which a passionate collector of books and manuscripts devoted to magic and witchcraft had discovered a volume which contained a painting of a small, hungry-looking dragon — behind which the artist had added a touch of artistic detail by putting in a cluttered heap of bones.

These were the bones which were later discovered in McKenzie Muir's basement after his house burned down above them — the mortal remains of no less than fifteen human beings, together with some larger bones whose origin was obscure.

The writer who wrote that story believed that writing was the greatest power in the world, and as Bob considered him and all the other writers who had labored hard all their lives to tell the truth as they understood it, he was genuinely outraged at the idea that Vadim Fedorov had been blacklisted by the Screenwriter's Guild, and that his grandson Ivan was facing the cancellation of his song for no reason other than that a malicious guy had claimed he'd done something he hadn't.

5

A Different Kind of Summer Project

Twenty minutes later, Bob and Mallory had arrived at the Salvage Yard where they were filling Jupiter in on what they'd discovered about Colton Clark. They'd checked him out on Facebook and Instagram and Twitter, and what they'd found wasn't pretty. Clark regularly bragged about his drinking exploits, subtly mentioned his drug use, and had a bad word to say about everyone. His posts were filled with swear words. He was a thoroughly disreputable and dislikable guy – though he was apparently the son of a United States Congressman, Douglas Clark.

At this last news, Jupiter's eyebrows shot up.

"That's very interesting," he said. "Tracey and Colton's father is Congressman Clark! The other day Mr. Szabó was telling me about a politician named Douglas Clark, but Clark is such a common name it never occurred to me that he could be Colton and Tracey's father. Maybe that was why Colton kept telling Ivan his father would get revenge –

and also how Colton got his arrest dismissed. Mr. Szabó is probably right that Douglas Clark let the power of his office go to his head."

"He said that about him?" Bob asked.

"He said that about all politicians, actually," Jupiter replied. "He implied that America was getting more and more like the country Fyodor and Marinka Fedorov fled. I hope it isn't, but when I talked to my aunt and uncle they agreed with Mr. Szabó that there was too much power in the hands of politicians who always wanted more and more of it."

Mallory's father, Callum, would certainly have agreed with that, she thought. So did she, actually. A *lot*. She distrusted politicians for the same reason she distrusted most policemen. They were *all* drawn to power.

As she and the others waited for Worthington to arrive to take them to the "book party," she felt surprisingly reluctant to show up at any such function. There was something distasteful about the almost universal hunger for public celebrations of private accomplishments, Mallory thought.

Of course, she understood why a writer like Cassandra Abelman would want to get publicity for a book she'd labored hard over, and finished, and seen published between two boards. Even so, since writing was a really private thing, and the relationship between the person who set words on a page and the person who read those words was also private, she couldn't get into the idea at all.

She also couldn't understand the idea of a writing group − especially one that had mostly female members, the way Cassandra's seemed to. On the whole, girls and women talked too much, and it was hard for Mallory to imagine anything more destructive to a good idea than to let a group of people loose on it. To Mallory, it seemed self-evident that creative ideas had to be nurtured in silence for a long time before they were shared.

Luckily, that didn't hold true for publicly available information, so when Worthington arrived, and she climbed into the front seat of the Flex, she had no trouble at all telling him what the case was when he asked. He was wearing sunglasses against the afternoon glare and he looked calm and dignified and handsome.

"Some git," Mallory replied − using a British term she knew Worthington would understand − "is claiming that our new client, Ivan Fedorov, stole a melody of his. He's claiming copyright infringement, though he hasn't filed the lawsuit yet. Ivan wrote the song and the most important part of the music for a new movie set in Russia during the time of Catherine the Great."

"Is the movie called *The Golden Age?*" Worthington asked.

"Yes," Mallory said. "I think it is."

"I was just reading about it," Worthington said. "Ever since my acting days, I've made it a point to keep up to date. Did you know that Per Jorgensen has quite an important role in it? He plays one of Catherine the Great's − well − lovers."

He glanced at her a bit anxiously, as if he was worried how she would react to this.

Though Mallory was surprised to hear that Per Jorgensen − a well-known Danish actor who she, The Three Investigators, and Worthington had all met the summer before in the course of a case − was acting in the movie Ivan Fedorov had written the song for, she was even more surprised that Worthington would try to shield her from the word 'lovers'.

She smiled. "Don't worry. I know what lovers are, Worthington. It's a really small world, isn't it? Especially in Hollywood. I wish I'd known Per Jorgensen was in the movie when we met Ivan and Cassandra. Maybe they know one another. Of course, Ivan isn't actually in the film, but he and Per Jorgensen will both have their names on it — at least if The Three Investigators can stop Colton's lawsuit!"

Worthington ran into some traffic downtown, and they arrived at Books & Bistro at twenty after five. Worthington said he was going to find a place to park and would be back to pick them up at 7:00, and after he left, Mallory and the boys stood on the sidewalk outside to gather themselves.

There was a blown-up portrait of Cassandra in the window, along with a sign advertising the book party and signing. In front of the sign was a big stack of thin books. The top one had a photo of a bungalow under the title *The House I Lived In*. As Mallory followed Jupiter, Pete, and Bob into Books & Bistro, the air was filled with the buzz of conversation.

Mallory could see that the bookstore was upscale, the lighting dim — the result of strategically placed pinspots. It was filled with little nooks created by the arrangement of bookshelves, encouraging browsing. Books were artfully arranged everywhere — on tables, in piles on the floor, tumbling and leaning on the shelves. In the back, beyond all the books,

Mallory caught a glimpse of the small bistro connected to the shop, where people sat hunched at café tables, eating.

The place was extraordinarily crowded, people everywhere, most of them dressed in business attire, as though they'd just come from the office – men wearing jackets and ties and women with makeup and dresses or blouses and skirts. They were all holding wine glasses and looking very pleased with themselves – with who they were and with how they had managed to be at a hip party such as this one.

In a general sense, Mallory agreed with Jupiter when it came to parties – she didn't like them – but this one struck her as more offensive than most, loud and jangly and filled with people who looked like they expected you to know who they were before you were introduced. Mallory was especially glad that she'd arrived with a cover story. It would be a lot easier to act a part than simply be herself.

She caught sight of Cassandra and Ivan across the room. Cassandra was sitting at a table signing copies of her book, and Ivan stood behind her looking a bit lost. He waved when he saw them and poked Cassandra and pointed. Mallory hoped they could tear themselves away from what they were doing and join them soon. She'd need them to point out Colton and Tracey. She and Bob had seen pictures of them on social media, but seeing people in person was different.

She looked at Jupiter, Bob, and Pete. Bob seemed anxious and stricken; Jupiter had assumed the air he usually took when acting, looking a lot dumber and less curious than he actually was – quite a good disguise. Only Pete was smiling and looking around avidly. Mallory assumed he was searching for the snacks.

"Did you see Ivan and Cassandra?" she said to the others. "They're over there." She pointed to the table.

"I really like them," Pete said, "and I think it's cool that they got married so young."

"I like them, too," Jupiter said, "but you can like them without thinking it's great they got married."

"But they seem so happy together!" Pete said.

"I agree," Mallory said. She did, too. "Besides, getting married young has been the norm throughout human history. Many people got married in their early teens. Think of Romeo and Juliet. That's historically accurate."

"Maybe," Jupiter said. "But just because people have always done something doesn't necessarily make it wise. We're just discovering that human brains are still developing, and plastic, until the age of twenty-five or so."

Mallory was a bit surprised at Jupiter's certainty. After all, she thought, even if what he said was true, why couldn't two people in love have plastic brains together?

They stopped talking when a couple of women pushed close to them and Mallory heard one of them mention the name Tracey Clark. She nodded urgently with her head toward the women and put her finger to her lips. The four of them stood a bit awkwardly, listening hard but trying to look like they weren't doing precisely what they *were* doing.

"She's not here yet," one of the women said. "But she will be. She wouldn't miss an opportunity to schmooze. She's really an operator. And not of heavy machinery."

Another woman laughed. "Tracey's not so bad," she said. "And she's gotten a *lot* better as a writer in the last six months."

Clearly, Mallory thought, these women were part of the writing group that Cassandra and Tracey belonged to. And it seemed that even the one who had said she wasn't all that bad didn't much like Tracey Clark. As for Mallory, though she knew little about her as of yet, she disliked the way her name was spelled with an "e" before the "y."

"I feel sorry for her ex," one of the women said. "She really took him to the cleaners."

"She's younger than I am!" another said. "She's only twenty-seven and already married and divorced. Slow down, girl."

Jupiter gave the rest of them a look as if to say, *See what I mean?*

"Her ex was already a successful businessman when she married him," one of the women said. "Do you think she planned to marry him and then divorce him, just to get half his money? Under the community property law, everything got divided fifty-fifty."

"It worked out so well for Tracey," one said, "you'd think her slimy father had written the law himself. When he was still just a local Congressman." They all laughed.

"That confirms it," Jupiter said quietly.

But Mallory was already eavesdropping again. It turned out that Tracey had gotten so much money in the divorce settlement that she'd been able to buy a house when she was only twenty-five, and now she was hoping to either make a lot of money with the novel she was writing or to marry another successful man. She was almost finished with the novel. She'd see how that went first.

Mallory had already disliked Colton Clark, but by this time she was starting to dislike Tracey too. She reminded herself that all this was opinion and hearsay. She'd meet Tracey soon, and until then she should give her the benefit of the doubt.

Now the women were talking about the novel Tracey was writing. "It's really *good*," one of them was saying. "And it keeps being good. Which is a surprise. Remember what she was writing when she first joined the group?"

"I sure do," another said. "All these 'hey girlfriend' stories, filled with brand names and pop culture references."

"And really awkward sentences," another said. "Boring and predictable and very up-to-the-minute L.A. This historical novel she's been working on is way better."

"She must have done a ton of research," the other woman said.

Mallory was trying to figure out what to think about this when she saw Ivan and Cassandra making their way through the crowd to join them. She and the others moved toward the couple, leaving the group of women behind.

"Hi!" Cassandra said. "Thanks so much

for coming. I hope it hasn't been too awful. These things can be very trying."

Jupiter smiled as if he agreed, but before he could say anything, Mallory jumped in.

"No," she said. "It's fine. After all, we're on a mission."

"I hope you've got your cover story straight," Ivan said, "because Tracey and Colton just walked in." He nodded toward the door where a young man and woman stood, surveying the crowd. "Over here," Ivan said. "You can get a better view."

Colton Clark squinted in the dimness of Books & Bistro. He was aggressively dressed for such a gathering − work boots, jeans, and an unbuttoned denim jacket over a white tee-shirt. His belt was thick, and a chain connected it to something in his front pocket. His pointed chin was dark with stubble, and his expression was sour. He stood with his hands on his hips, as if daring anyone to talk to him.

To Mallory, his sister hardly looked like she was related to him. She'd been wearing dark glasses but she put them away in the large leather bag that hung from her shoulder. She was wearing a summery dress, in a pastel flower print, and she looked quite attractive and poised. Her hair was blond, cut short in a bob. She looked, Mallory thought, like a majority of the young professional women at the party in terms of style and attitude — though there was something a bit hard-edged about her cheekbones and jawline.

"We'll leave you," Cassandra said hurriedly. "No reason to let them see us together. Good luck."

When the four of them were alone again, Jupiter pulled them close.

"Mallory and I should handle this, I think," he said. "Bob and Pete, you're not the best actors in the world."

"You can say that again," Bob said, looking vastly relieved.

"So you guys hang back," Jupiter said, "and we'll see what we can find out." To Mallory, he said, "Since we're high school students, we might find a way to get Colton talking about high school. But I guess we have to start by asking Tracey about her writing group. You should do that, then I'll try to handle Colton."

Before Colton and Tracey could split up or start talking to other people, Jupiter went right up to them, Mallory following close behind him.

"Are you Tracey Clark?" Jupiter asked her. "Someone pointed you out to me."

Tracey looked surprised. "Why yes," she said. "Who are you?"

Jupiter introduced himself and Mallory as two high school students from Rocky Beach, embarked on a summer project about the media.

"We heard you were in Cassandra Abelman's writing group and that you're at work on a novel," Mallory said, remembering the mission Jupiter had given her. "Could we ask you some questions about publishing?"

"Certainly," Tracey said. "Thanks for asking – though, so far, the only stuff I've published has been online."

Jupiter turned to Colton who was looking at him and Mallory with disdain. He kept craning his neck, looking for who knew what, and he seemed sullen and hostile. Mallory couldn't imagine why he'd come, but Jupiter proceeded with his plan.

"Did you have a media class at your high school?" he asked Colton. "When did you graduate? Were you in any clubs?"

Colton rolled his eyes. He nudged his sister. "I'm out of here," he said. "If you want me, look for the free eats and drinks."

"You'll have to excuse my brother," Tracey said to Jupiter. "I really do apologize.

Colton's got a lot to learn about politeness."

Mallory could see that Jupiter was as disappointed as she was that Colton had effected such a quick escape, but there seemed nothing to do now but talk to Tracey, as if she and Jupiter really *were* doing research. She took out a small pad of paper and a pencil so she could pretend to take notes.

"Could you tell us something about whatever you're working on right now?" she asked.

Tracey seemed to compose her face before beginning. "It's a sort of departure for me," she said. "I was writing contemporary stories, and I wasn't very happy with them. I decided to get more ambitious, so I'm writing a long historical novel, in the third person. It's been a challenge, but I've learned so much!"

Mallory jotted down a few quick words and then asked, rather desperately, "I'm always interested in how writers work. Do you write long-hand? At a keyboard? What process do you use? Do you write in one long file, or in bits and pieces and then put them together later?"

Mallory thought these questions were intensely stupid, but when Tracey answered, it was clear she didn't.

"That's an interesting question," Tracey said. "Your last one. I actually like to work in one long file. It makes it easier to search for things. But it's scary, too. Like, what if everything I've written got lost or erased? So every day, before I start, I duplicate the file from the previous day."

"That's a great idea!" Mallory said, wishing Jupiter would help her out with this. At the moment, he was standing with his hands in his pockets, letting her take the lead.

Tracey smiled graciously. "I think so, too," she said. "That way I save everything I've done, and even if I change some of it, I still have a perfect copy of the way it was – in case I change my mind later and want to go back to the original."

"But you must have a lot of files," Mallory said, glancing at Jupiter in what she hoped was an urgent silent plea for help. He didn't seem to notice.

"I do," Tracey said. "For the book I'm working on I have something like four hundred files – each one a little longer than the one before it. I try to write – or rewrite – three or four pages a day. I think the book will be about 700 pages long when I'm done with it."

"700 pages?" Mallory asked, suddenly

getting interested in this conversation. "How do you keep all the files straight?"

"The files are all automatically dated, of course," Tracey said, "and though I may look at an earlier file, I'm careful to make all the changes in the current one. And I use a small handheld tape recorder as well. I keep audio files. I dictate what I think might happen next in the book as a way of keeping the process flowing."

Mallory was jostled from behind, and she turned to see that Colton had returned, drink in hand. But he ignored her and Jupiter and spoke directly to Tracey. "Hey, Tracey," he said. "I just ran into Disco."

Tracey frowned. "What's he doing here?"

"He thought I might be here," Colton said. "You gotta help out. He just got caught trying to steal a guitar or something from the back of a van parked outside. He wasn't caught by a cop, just some nosy parker, but the nosy parker had a nosy parker friend and they've got him jammed up."

"I don't like your friends," Tracey said. "Too many of them are creeps. And thieves."

"Yeah, yeah," Colton said dismissively. "But come along, will ya?" He looked at her strangely, as if she had no choice.

"You'll have to excuse me," Tracey said to Mallory and Jupiter. "It's been very nice talking to you. Good luck with your paper."

She let herself be drawn away by her brother. Mallory followed them with her eyes and saw Pete and Bob coming to meet them.

"Well?" Pete said excitedly. "Did you learn anything?"

"Not really," Mallory said, "except that you were right to warn Ivan not to be so careless about his van. Apparently some low-life friend of Colton Clark just tried to steal a guitar from the back of it. Some good guys caught him. The thing I can't understand is why Tracey Clark agreed to help Colton talk the good guys out of calling the cops."

"I wondered that, too," Jupiter said. "It almost seemed as if Tracey was under her brother's thumb. As if he had something on her."

"Like what?" asked Pete.

"I have no idea," Jupiter said. "But I disliked her more than I expected to – almost as much as I disliked her brother. As we all overheard, she's leveraged a brief marriage into enough money to buy herself a house. And her brother is a classic leech – a freeloader. With what Ivan told us about Colton threatening him with his father, I imagine Congressman Clark has given his children some seriously twisted ideas about life."

"That's probably true," Pete said. "But if that's all you've learned, then we really didn't need to come to this party at all, did we?"

"Maybe not," Jupiter said. "Though you never know beforehand what may later prove crucial to an investigation."

Since the four of them had nothing else to do at the moment, when Pete suggested they go find the snacks and drinks, the rest of them followed him. They ate and drank for a while, and then Mallory looked around to see that people were leaving and the party was beginning to wind down. Cassandra and Ivan found them and asked if they'd had any luck with Colton.

"Not yet," Jupiter admitted, "but I've rarely met anyone I disliked more intensely – except maybe his sister – and I hope we can find a way to wipe the sneer off his face."

Worthington, reliable as always, was waiting at the curb, and after the four of them climbed in, he followed Ivan and Cassandra's van through the maze of streets and avenues that led from the bookstore to their house. Ivan pulled into the driveway and Worthington parked on the street just long enough for Mallory and the others to get out.

"Do you want to come in?" Jupiter asked Worthington.

"No, thank you," Worthington said. "There's a restaurant in this neighborhood I've always loved. I'm going to eat there, but I'll be back to pick you up at 9:30."

Ivan and Cassandra's house had a boxy shape, a hip roof with a cupola in the exact middle, long dormer windows on the second floor, and a front porch that ran the entire width of the house. It was on a small lot in a quiet neighborhood, near the end of a cul de sac, and the minute Mallory saw it, she loved it.

"Come in, come in," Cassandra called from the porch as the four of them, led by Mallory, walked up the steps. The front door opened onto the living room, which ran the width of the house, just like the porch. There was a tiled fireplace on one end and an area with shelves holding books and a large collection of DVDs on the other. The walls were hung with vintage movie posters. In front of the shelves was a low wooden cabinet with drawers that held a large flat-screen TV, set catty-corner.

Behind the living room were four rooms – the dining room and kitchen to the left, and Ivan's music room and Cassandra's study to the right. When Cassandra saw how much Mallory liked the house, she told her that it was a classic bungalow design called an American Four Square, and that it was actually what was called a 'kit house' – built from ready-to-put-together pieces from a company in southern California.

"A kit house?" said Mallory. "I really like it!"

Soon Ivan was ordering pizza, and soon after that, they all had a soda and were sitting on a couch and chairs arranged at the fireplace end of the living room. Pete couldn't resist telling Ivan the story about the low-life friend of Colton's who'd been caught trying to steal a guitar out of his van, right on the street in front of Books & Bistro.

Ivan looked astonished. "I should have been more careful," he said. "But it's really hard for me to imagine people wanting to steal things that aren't theirs. I know that's stupid. Really stupid – especially in a city like L.A."

"Or anywhere," said Jupiter. Mallory saw that he realized he might have been rude to say that, so he added, "Not stupid, but un-wise. A lot of human beings are pretty weak when it comes to resisting the temptation to freeload off of other people."

"That's so true," Ivan said. "And since that's exactly what Colton Clark has been try-ing to do with the music I wrote for *The Golden Age*, I should have been more on my guard."

"I really don't see how you could have been on your guard against a false accusation of copyright infringement!" Cassandra said protectively.

"I couldn't have guarded against that, of course," Ivan said, smiling at Cassandra, "but at least I could have checked to make sure I'd locked my van!"

"So tell me," Cassandra said, changing the subject and turning to Jupiter and Mallory. "What did you learn from Colton and Tracey?"

"Nothing from Colton," Mallory said. "He was too busy getting free drinks and hang-ing out with his hoodlum friend. But Tracey told us something about the book she's writing and the process she uses. I take it she's working on a historical novel."

Cassandra nodded. "That's right," she said. "It's a third person narrative about a woman who was born in Russia and came to the United States after the Russian Revolution."

"That's quite a coincidence, isn't it?" Jupiter said.

Cassandra glanced at Ivan. She looked a bit embarrassed. "I'm afraid Tracey may have gotten the idea from me. Or not from me, exactly, but from the story I told her about Ivan and his family. Of course she's done a lot of research. She started the novel about a month after she joined the writing group. She wrote short stories before."

"So we heard," Jupiter said drily.

"Anyway, when she asked me about Ivan, I told her all about the Fedorovs – how Ivan's great-grandfather came over after the Revolution, about his grandfather and the lost novel – "

"The lost novel?" Bob said.

"Yes," Cassandra said. "We learned that Ivan's grandfather, who wrote mysteries, had been working on a literary novel for a long, long time. But after he died, no one could find a copy. We have no idea what happened to it."

"I don't remember Vadim, unfortunately," Ivan said. "I was only three when he died. But when I was older, my father told me about the book."

"What did he tell you?" Mallory asked.

"That it started in Russia before the Revolution and followed a couple a lot like Vadim's mother and father who escaped and came to California," Ivan said. "As Cassandra told you, he worked hard on it for many years; at least that's what my father said. He wanted to get it right."

Jupiter sat forward in his chair, interested and intent in a way he hadn't been before. "And you said that the book was not to be found in his papers after he died?"

"That's right," Ivan said. "Which is particularly too bad, because he left the book to me in his will, and if it had been a big success, it would have set me and Cassandra up for life!"

He grinned and poked Cassandra, who smiled.

Mallory knew he was joking, but there was still an undertone of sadness in his voice. What would it be like to have a wonderful novel about your family left to you in your grandfather's will and then have it disappear before you'd even had a chance to read it?

All of a sudden someone pounded on the door, three times, hard – much harder than

necessary, Mallory thought. She jumped, and
so did everyone else. Her first thought, irra-
tional though it was, was that one of Colton's
violent friends had followed them to the house
and was now demanding entry!

6

A Long-Lost Book

Jupiter was also startled by the pounding, but he realized almost instantly that it was the delivery man with the pizzas. He settled back in his chair as Ivan went to the door.

Though he'd said nothing about it, and had tried his best to hide how he was feeling, he couldn't remember an afternoon and evening that had been such a complete waste of time. They'd learned nothing from Colton Clark or his sister that would help them prevent the threatened lawsuit, and though the conversation they'd had since arriving at Ivan and Cassandra's house had been unobjectionable, it hadn't moved things forward in terms of their investigation.

He'd been silently lamenting the fact that he'd allowed himself to be swayed by his kind feelings toward Mrs. Vasiliev when the phrase "lost novel" had entered the conversation. At that, Jupiter immediately snapped to attention.

On the drive from Rocky Beach to Los Angeles, Bob had elaborated on his talk with Hector Sebastian, but he hadn't gone into detail, and he certainly hadn't talked about a lost novel that Vadim Fedorov had been writing. Why hadn't he published it while he was alive? Why had he left it to Ivan? And where had it gotten to? Jupiter wondered.

As he sat ruminating on these questions, he reflected that Ivan had had many years to get used to the situation, and he certainly didn't seem perturbed by the fact of the book's disappearance. Obviously what he'd said about the book setting him up for life had been an attempt at a joke. But Jupiter, who had investigated a good number of mysteries by this point in his almost fifteen years, knew one when he saw one, and there was something quite peculiar about this story.

Ivan's grandfather, a well-known writer of apparently excellent mystery novels, had also written a literary novel the world had never seen. He had left it to his grandson in his will, but after his death it was never found. Where could it have gone? Jupiter wondered. Could it have been thrown out accidentally, or lost when the papers were boxed and moved? Could Vadim Fedorov, frail and possibly of unsound mind at the end, have decided it was no good and destroyed it before he died? What if, somehow, it had been stolen?

Jupiter steepled his fingers and smiled. Let's be honest, he thought to himself. The other mystery – the one about finding proof that Ivan was the real writer of the song in *The Golden Age,* and that that surly creep Colton Clark had no claim on it – wasn't very exciting. At least not very exciting when compared to a missing manuscript that was supposed to be Ivan's.

"Four pizzas," Ivan announced as he returned from the door. "Tomato and cheese, sausage and peppers, pepperoni, and the kitchen sink. Cassandra, do you want to eat in the dining room?"

"Yes," Cassandra said. "I've already put plates and napkins on the table. I'll get silverware for anyone who wants it. Does anyone need another drink?"

"Me, please," Pete said.

Jupiter was only moderately fond of pizza and tended to eat his with a knife and fork. But when a steaming slice of tomato and cheese had been put before him, it looked excellent. He found he was quite hungry, but even as he began to eat, he wondered how he could find out more about the missing novel.

What he really wanted, he had to admit – if only to himself – was to make the mystery they'd been hired to solve more interesting by engaging with another mystery at the same time. But he also realized that it might be better to approach his subject sideways and not focus too intently on the lost book.

"This is great pizza!" Pete said enthusiastically. Everyone but Jupiter had picked up their slice, and for a moment he felt a little prim, cutting bite-sized pieces with his knife and fork. He was amazed at how fast Pete's slice of pepperoni was disappearing into his mouth.

Jupiter wiped his mouth with the napkin. "Obviously," he began, talking to Ivan and Cassandra, "the four of us are not really writing a paper about the Fedorov family, but I'd like to pretend for the moment that we *are*. Sooner or later, we'll be talking to classmates of yours who were also at that graduation party where you supposedly stole Colton's song, and it might be excellent cover for the interviews."

Mallory looked at him a little oddly, as though she knew something was up.

"So it would be great," Jupiter went on, "if you could tell us a little more about your family, Ivan."

"Sure!" Ivan said cheerfully.

"Maybe you could start with the book

you were meant to inherit," Jupiter said, as nonchalantly as possible.

"O.K.," said Ivan. "As I told you, I was only three when my grandfather died, so of course I knew nothing about any inheritance or any book for the longest time. In fact, I didn't learn about it until I was fifteen. One day my father said he wanted to talk to me, then sat me down and very seriously told me his father had left me some money in his will and that it would become mine when I turned 21. He hadn't wanted me to know when I was younger, because he'd been afraid that if I grew up expecting a windfall, I wouldn't work hard or be ambitious and might develop a set of shallow and superficial values.

"He may even have been right, I don't know. Some of the kids I went to high school with – the ones who had trust funds they'd inherit – were people I generally disliked. They acted as though they deserved what was coming to them, no matter what.

"Anyway," Ivan went on, "my twenty-first year was complicated. My father died, which was brutal, and my grandfather's bequest came to me, for which I was very, very grateful. It let me and Cassandra buy this house, after we were married."

"That must have been a lot of money," Pete said. "I mean, this is a great house."

"It wasn't enough to buy the house outright," Ivan said, "but we were able to put down a sizable down payment and get a mortgage for the rest."

"We were very lucky," Cassandra said. "You can hardly believe how much houses cost in this section of L.A. Tracey Clark bought a house not all that far from here, by the way – though from all the gossip I've heard, she was able to buy hers because of a huge divorce settlement."

"We heard her ex-husband was a successful businessman," Mallory said.

"Yes," Cassandra said. "I think that's true. Anyway – " She reached across the table and touched Ivan's arm.

She sat back in her chair. "And what Ivan said before just isn't right," she said. "Ivan would never have developed the wrong values; he just doesn't have it in him. He's honest and he's true, which is what makes his music so special. That's why we're so upset about this thing with Colton Clark. The suggestion that Ivan's song isn't really his is bad enough, but to suggest that Ivan is the kind of person who would even *consider* doing something like that is worse."

Yes, Jupiter thought. He was sure that was correct. But his interests lay elsewhere at the moment.

"So," he said to Ivan, "when your father told you about the money – is that also when you found out about the book?"

"That's right," Ivan said. "He'd never mentioned it before, which I thought was a little strange. But then it turned out that, though my grandfather had left the manuscript to me, there *was* no manuscript. My father had no explanation. For a while I was obsessed with the idea of the book, and I asked my father about it practically every chance I got. He said his father had been very secretive about it and had never even shown a page of it to him. All Dad really knew was a few basic facts – some of the book took part in Russia, before and during the Revolution; some of it took part in Hollywood during the golden age of film – "

Mallory interrupted. "That's an odd coincidence. Isn't the movie you wrote the song for called *The Golden Age*?"

Ivan laughed. "That's right. As it turns out, there were lots of golden ages – always named by people looking back on them nostalgically. The movie I wrote the song for is about

Catherine the Great and the supposed golden age of Russia."

"And the Danish actor Per Jorgensen plays one of Catherine the Great's lovers?" Mallory asked, to Jupiter's surprise. He and the others had met Per Jorgensen on a case the summer before and although they hadn't seen him since, he stood out in Jupiter's mind as a vivid and interesting human being.

Before Jupiter could turn to Mallory and ask how she knew that Per was in the movie, Ivan said, "Yes, he does. He's great."

"I thought so, too," said Mallory. "We met him last summer on a case."

"You did?" asked Ivan in amazement.

"Yes," Mallory said. "We were at his house the night we caught this terrible German fraud trying to steal a painting by Edvard Munch. How well do you know him?"

"Not well at all," Ivan said. "We just met a couple of times in the sound studio, but he was complimentary about my music, and I told him how much I liked his work. I didn't mention this Colton Clark thing, of course."

"Of course not," Jupiter said. "I liked Per Jorgensen, too, but could you just finish your story about the lost novel?" He sounded a little impatient, even to himself.

Ivan nodded and went on.

"Anyway, my father told me that all his father really told him was that the two main characters were based on my great-grandfather and great-grandmother, Fyodor and Marinka, and that there was a section about the filming of a movie that resembled the movie for which my great-grandfather won an Oscar."

"Would that be *Dawn over Petrograd?*" Jupiter said. "Mallory and I read that he won Best Supporting Actor for his role."

"Yes," Ivan said. "Have you seen it? The weirdest thing about it is the way it portrays the Russian Revolution. According to the movie, it was somewhere between a senior prom and a birthday party – all gay and festive, with happy dancing peasants and lots of balalaikas and cheery celebrations, more or less following the Bolshevik line that the 1917 revolution was a happy day for all humankind.

"With my family history, I know a good deal about it, and I can promise you it wasn't like that at all. By 1937, Joseph Stalin was responsible for the deaths of more than two million Russians. From what I've read, it's hard to really communicate the horror of being forced to conform to such a murderous regime. The Soviet system didn't just kill peoples' bodies. It murdered their minds and their souls. It managed to suck all the joy and excitement out of life. And, of course, it made it almost impossible to be an artist. All that writers and painters were allowed to produce was pro-Soviet propaganda."

Ivan sighed, then shrugged and took a bite of his pizza.

"Luckily, that's all over now," he added. "Russia is Russia again. In case you don't know, Feodor and Fyodor are just different ways to spell the same Russian name in English. My great-grandfather's name – Fyodor Fedorov – means Theodore, son of Theodore. The son named after the father – often the case in Russia. The suffix -ov or -vich means 'son of.'

"But after the family left Russia, it abandoned the patronymic and stuck with 'Fedorov.' Otherwise my father's name would have been Yuri Vadimov." He grinned. "And my name would have been Ivan Yurinov. Which would have been most unfortunate."

Everyone laughed, Pete especially. "Yurinov," he said. "That's hilarious."

There were a few pieces of pizza left, but when Ivan offered them around, everyone said they had already eaten too much.

"But it was so good!" Pete said. Groaning happily, he got to his feet and helped with the cleanup, carrying the empty pizza boxes to the trash and putting the plates and silverware on the counter next to the sink in the kitchen. Then they all moved back to the living room.

"It's a little warm for this," Ivan said, gesturing toward the fireplace, "but a fire is always so cheerful, and most of the heat will go right up the chimney. Should I light one?"

Jupiter's firm opinion was no, but everyone else thought this was a fine idea, and in no time a small fire was crackling merrily in the fireplace. Cassandra had opened the windows wide, and the cool evening air flowed in.

When they had settled back into their seats, Jupiter asked, "Was it unusual in Hollywood in those days for a pro-Soviet film to be made?"

"That's an interesting question," Ivan said. "There were lots of Russian émigrés in Hollywood — both pro- and anti-Communist. Some, like my great-grandfather, knew that the Soviet Union had become a terrible, repressive place and that Communism was a disaster. But others wanted to believe the Bolshevik propaganda — that Russia under Communism had become a happy utopia.

"*Dawn over Petrograd* came from the utopians, but my great-grandfather needed to work. So he signed on to play someone he would have hated and disagreed with fiercely – a heroic Bolshevik. But he was such a good actor that he played the role with conviction, and later on, there were lots of people who confused him with the character."

"That was what Mallory and I concluded," Jupiter said, nodding.

Cassandra had been listening without interrupting, but now she said to Ivan, "Tell them about the clues that the Fyodor character supposedly wove into the movie without the director knowing."

At this remark, Jupiter pricked up his ears.

"That's right," Ivan said. "My father told me that my grandfather had added certain sorts of actions to his role – actions that would let you know that the actor hated Bolsheviks, even though he was playing one. Apparently Fyodor had a friend on the set – a fellow Russian who also hated Communism – who conspired with him."

"That's a fascinating story," Jupiter said. "You've seen it, of course. Did you watch it with an eye toward uncovering the clues, whatever they are?"

"We did," Cassandra said. "We've watched it several times. But we really couldn't find anything useful. We kept pointing at the screen and saying, 'There! There!' But each time it turned out to be nothing."

Jupiter nodded. He understood. It would be quite a challenge to look for hidden clues in a movie. But he was up for it.

"Do you know where we could get a copy of the movie?" he asked.

"You can borrow our copy if you want," Ivan said. "It's one of the films my father gave to me. Maybe if the four of you watch it, you'll have an easier time than Cassandra and I had."

He got up, walked to the other end of the room where the books and DVDs were kept, hunkered down, and studied the spines. He plucked out a jewel case and returned with it. "Here you go," he said, handing it to Jupiter. "Good luck."

"I'll take good care of it," Jupiter said. "I promise."

He turned to Cassandra. "If I'm remembering correctly," he said, "when we met at Mrs. Vasiliev's apartment, you mentioned that you and Ivan first met because your father had interviewed Ivan's father, Yuri."

"That's right," Cassandra said, looking impressed. "You have a very good memory."

"That's why he's the First Investigator," Pete said proudly.

"Do you think it would be possible for us to meet your father?" Jupiter asked Cassandra.

"Sure," Cassandra said. "I could set up an appointment."

"That would be great," Jupiter said. "Could you tell us a little bit more about him?"

"His name is Jason Abelman," she said. "He's been a film buff since he was a boy. He went to U.C.L.A. where he studied film history, and now he's the director of the American Film History Library. He has an office there, where he spends most of his time. It's pretty close to Rocky Beach – about fifteen or twenty minutes away, depending on traffic. Could you meet him there?"

"I'm sure we could," Jupiter said.

"I'll text him after you leave," she said, "and see if he's available sometime tomorrow morning, and if he is, I'll let you know."

"We're free tomorrow morning, yes?" he asked, looking from Bob, to Pete, to Mallory. All of them nodded yes. He turned back to Cassandra. "That will be fine," he said. "We'll look forward to meeting him if he can see us."

"How will that help with the Colton Clark mess?" Ivan asked.

Ah, Jupiter thought. Caught out. "It won't help directly, I'm afraid," he said, "but in a case like this, the more information we can gather, the better off we are. And by the way, since you've reminded me, it might be good if you could give us the names of anyone you remember who was at that graduation party that's at the center of the dispute. Anyone who saw you and would remember you and could support your side of the story."

"Sure," Ivan said. As he began to speak, Jupiter could see that Bob, out of habit, had found a small notepad in his pocket and was poised to write down anything Ivan said.

Ivan closed his eyes and sank back in his chair, trying to conjure up names and faces from over five years before. "You could ask Frank Tancredi," he said, "and Billy Osterman, if you can find them. They were there and probably stayed after I left. The girl who threw the party was Helene Bobinsky, but she's married now and I don't know her married name."

"Maybe she didn't change her name," Cassandra said. "I didn't."

"That's true," Ivan said, smiling. "You could also try to find Harriet Rush. And maybe Harold Greenmore and Sissy Bobek. They were a couple. In fact, they might still be together."

"Got it, Bob?" Jupiter asked.

"Got it," Bob said confidently.

"If you think of any other names," Jupiter said, "please let us know."

There was another knock at the door, not nearly as aggressive as the pizza guy's knock had been. Jupiter glanced at his watch. It was Worthington, right on time. He got to his feet.

"That's our ride," he said. "I guess we'd better get going."

The others all got up as Ivan went to the door and let Worthington in, and there was a flurry of handshakes and thank yous.

"You're more than welcome," Ivan said. "Cassandra and I are really happy to have met you."

"Likewise," said Mallory, including all of them in her comment. "Congratulations again, Cassandra, on your new book."

"Thanks very much," Cassandra said, "and thanks again for coming to the party."

Jupiter was quiet most of the way back

home, as he thought about everything that had happened. Everyone else was quiet too. It seemed they'd all had enough talking and socializing to last a while. They were just about back to the Rocky Beach town limits when Jupiter spoke.

"Do the three of you have any ideas about how we should proceed with the case?" he asked. He thought it best that he not tip his hand about his interest in the missing book.

"Usually you tell *us* how we'll proceed," Mallory said. "You don't normally ask us. What's up?"

Jupiter smiled. Mallory was very sharp; he was glad she was working with them full time now.

"I know what we *should* be doing," Bob said. "Looking for the people whose names Ivan just gave us and tracking them down and talking to them. I'm sure a bunch of them will support Ivan's and Cassandra's story. But I've gotten really interested in the whole Fedorov family saga. It'll be great if Mr. Abelman is able to see us, and we can find out what he knows. We could even ask him about this lost book. It's almost like a hidden treasure, and we've gotten pretty good at finding those."

"Yes!" Pete said. "Even if it's only a

book."

"Only a book!" Bob said. "There's nothing more valuable than a book. If it's the right book, of course. A good book."

"But how can you know before you read it if it is or it isn't?" Pete asked.

"You can't," said Mallory. "That's why it's so important to never let anyone get rid of books – to censor them or burn them, or any of the other terrible things people have done to books since they were first invented. Because you can't know, until you read them yourself, what's really in them."

"Anyway, I think this means we all agree with you, Jupiter," Bob said. "We're all interested in the missing book."

"Of course," Jupiter said, "we should also try to locate the people whose names Ivan gave us. We don't need a lot of people, but if we can find three or four who support Ivan, I expect we can get Colton Clark to see he has no chance of winning a lawsuit."

He paused and looked out the window at the houses they were passing. There were lights in every one, though the curtains and drapes had been drawn, and all he could see were shadowy figures – if he could see anyone at all. He was glad to hear that his friends were also intrigued by the idea of Vadim Fedorov's missing novel.

Worthington dropped Bob off first, and then Pete, and then Mallory. As they said good night, Jupiter promised he'd call first thing in the morning if he heard from Cassandra and they had an appointment at the American Film History Library with Mr. Abelman. He then climbed into the passenger seat, next to Worthington, for the short ride back to the Salvage Yard.

"A profitable evening, Master Jones?" Worthington said, with a raised eyebrow and a sly tone. He only called Jupiter "Master Jones" these days when the two of them were alone.

Jupiter laughed. "Maybe, Worthington," he said. "We'll have to see where it leads. I know it's short notice, but we may need a ride to the American Film History Library in Boxwood tomorrow morning. Is there any way you could drive us?"

Worthington said, "As far as I can remember, my schedule is open tomorrow morning. Just give me a ring when you know for sure."

Jupiter said good night to Worthington and thanked him again. The Salvage Yard was dark and quiet, as was Jupiter's house, behind the tall wooden fence at the back. His aunt and uncle always went to bed early, and he didn't expect to see them.

The streetlights outside the Salvage Yard cast long and spooky shadows, and Jupiter was suddenly self-conscious about how loud his feet sounded as he walked across the gravel. He let himself through the gate at the back that led to his house and mounted the steps to the porch.

It *had* been a profitable evening, he thought. A case that had seemed a bit dreary had suddenly grabbed his interest. Still carrying the DVD of *Dawn over Petrograd*, he opened the front door quietly and was tiptoeing toward the stairs when he tripped over something on the floor and almost fell headlong. Whatever it was was made of metal and made a loud clanging.

"Jupiter?" his aunt's querulous voice called from upstairs. "Jupiter? Is that you? Watch out for that pile of curtain rods," she called. "I just finished cutting them this evening. They're all ready for you to put up. Do you see them?"

"Yes," he said. "I see them." He didn't tell her that they had almost caused him to break his neck, but, on a sudden impulse, he *did* say, "I'm going to Headquarters for a minute," then left the house again, went to

Headquarters, and booted up the firm's old desktop computer. He wanted to see what kind of facilities the American Film History Library had available, and when he discovered that the place had a screening room on which to show old movies, he decided that — if possible — that was where he wanted The Three Investigators to screen *Dawn Over Petrograd*.

7

An Encounter With Tracey Clark

Bob had gotten the call from Jupiter right at breakfast the following morning.

"Mr. Abelman can meet with us," Jupiter had told him. "We don't have a firm appointment, but we should get over there this morning. He said he'd fit us in after we got there."

Now Bob and the others were at the Salvage Yard, waiting for Worthington again. While they waited, Bob suggested that they use the time to see if they could locate any of the people Ivan had mentioned the night before.

"I think we should limit the search to southern California," he said.

"I agree," said Jupiter. "That way whoever we find can be interviewed in person and would be easily available if they were called to make a formal statement. But I've been thinking about the way Colton treated me and Mallory last night, and I'm not at all certain that Cassandra was right about us seeming less threatening because we're high school students. I'm afraid they may simply dismiss us altogether, the way Colton did, just because we're young."

"You might be right," Mallory said. "Also, they might be a lot more cooperative if they thought there was something in it for them. Let's see what we can find out, though."

Bob and Mallory sat in the outdoor workshop, their laptops open, going down the list Bob had written on his notepad the night before.

Searching for people on the Internet was tedious, Bob thought, but certainly easier than it had been when the only way to find someone was by physically searching public records or going door-to-door and following leads. Of the names Ivan had given, it turned out only three were still local and had e-mails and phone numbers listed online.

"We've got three, Jupiter," Mallory reported. "At least three we have contact information for. Who knows if they'll be helpful."

"I'll see if I can find a list of Ivan's graduating class," Bob said. He worked quickly and soon located an article congratulating the class of 2015 at Roosevelt High. It ended with a list of the graduates' names. He and Mallory worked down the list until they had the contact information for four more people. It didn't take

136

long.

"Seven ought to be plenty to start with," Bob said. "Don't you think?"

"Yes," Jupiter said.

"That's a relief," Pete said. "At least we've done *something* that has to do with the case we're supposed to be working on!"

Bob agreed with him, and so did Mallory and Jupiter.

Since Worthington still hadn't arrived, Bob turned back to the research he'd been doing on and off about the Fedorov family. He found them fascinating.

This time he turned his attention to Ivan's father Yuri, the one in the line of Fedorov men they knew the least about. All they really knew was that he'd died of lung cancer several years before, and that he'd been interviewed by Jason Abelman.

Bob was interested to discover that Yuri Fedorov had begun his professional life as a serious composer. He'd written a series of string quartets and piano sonatas before he shifted gears.

The article didn't say whether Yuri was displeased with his earlier efforts or needed to make more money, but for whatever reason, he began composing for the movies. Soon he was writing the soundtracks for major films and had been quite successful.

He'd been dashing and handsome, and, as a young man, a bit of a playboy – spending money freely and having a series of relationships that lasted only a year or two. He didn't settle down and get married until after he'd turned forty. He was forty-seven when his only son Ivan was born. He'd divorced Ivan's mother when the boy was two.

Bob was intrigued by the fact that the patrilineal Fedorov line had resulted in four serious artists in four generations. Bob's mother was an evolutionary biologist, and he wondered what she would make of that. Did she think that creativity itself was at least partially heritable? Or was it a result of being young and impressionable and growing up in a household where art was taken seriously and your first role model was an artist?

But beyond that, Bob pondered the fact – and not for the first time – that the lives of writers – of artists of all kinds really – had a special appeal for him.

And obviously not just for him – for a lot of people. It was no wonder that someone had established the American Film History Museum to celebrate the art of film and the highly unusual collaboration of all sorts of artists — writers, set designers, costume designers, composers, cinematographers, directors — it took to make it happen.

Bob didn't think he'd like working in the film industry much. It seemed a bit chaotic and involved crowds of people. While he was very good at collaboration when it came to working with Mallory, Pete, and Jupiter, they were his best friends, and otherwise, in general, Bob liked working alone. He was rarely happier than when he was turning his notes from the various cases into accounts of them for The Three Investigators' website.

The only way he'd ever be able to be an artist, he thought, was if he really *did* become a writer — maybe someone like Hector Sebastian or Vadim Fedorov — though he also sometimes thought that maybe he'd like to be a historian instead.

Bob was just closing his laptop when Worthington arrived, and they were soon all in the Flex again, heading for their meeting with Mr. Abelman. On the way, Bob talked with the others about what to do next on the case itself.

"Now that we have a list of seven people from Ivan's class, along with their e-mails and phone numbers," he said, "I think the next logical step is to send them each an e-mail, asking if they were at Helene Bobinski's party and if we can talk to them."

"That's a good idea," Pete said. "You can send out the same letter to each of them. And remember to ask if they remember Ivan and Colton at the party. That might save us a little work."

They arrived at the library much more quickly than Bob had thought they would, but the traffic was light and there had been no delays. The building was on a hilltop, with a parking lot to the side. It had been designed by a modern architect, and it looked like other buildings Bob had seen before − a big glass box, with vertical steel beams running at intervals from the base to the flat roof, three stories above.

It wasn't Bob's kind of building at all, but Worthington said that he'd been there before, and that it was actually great inside. He said a lot of people in the film industry went there, and as a result sometimes regular people came just to see if they could catch a glimpse of someone famous.

Worthington went with them as they entered the atrium, and after climbing a set of graduated granite steps, Bob could see that the place had a lot to recommend it. The space where they stood was open all the way to the ceiling – which was studded with skylights, so it was open to the sky. Shafts of sunlight pierced the room. Several large trees in huge planters reached upwards, and there were comfortable chairs to sit in.

The Circulation Desk was behind a glass wall, to the side, and behind it were open stacks made of gleaming metal strut channels and black matte shelves, running all the way to the back of the library. Bob could see people walking up and down, browsing.

Above were two more stories of stacks, also open, with a steel railing at the front, forming a sort of double mezzanine. They had been ingeniously designed so they seemed to be floating in the air. On either side of the long curved Circulation Desk were two glass elevators that accessed the upper floors.

To the right was an elegant small screening room – a raked auditorium with limited seating, where films were shown between the hours of 9:00 and 4:00 – except on Wednesdays, when the library was closed, or when there was no one there who wanted to see the day's movies.

The schedule was listed on a board at

the door. Today, silent films — *Sunrise: A Tale of Two Humans, The General, Nosferatu.* Tomorrow, film noir — *Double Indemnity, The Big Sleep, In A Lonely Place.* The notice said that the room was also available for private screenings in the event that it wasn't being otherwise used.

Two hallways on either side of the screening room led to offices. Bob supposed Mr. Abelman was down one of them. On the walls were framed posters of movies, going all the way back to the beginnings of Hollywood.

The five of them ducked into the screening room where *Sunrise* was currently playing and took seats in the back. The room was sparsely filled, one person here, a couple there. It took a while for Bob's eyes to get accustomed to the dark. The seats were highly upholstered and very comfortable.

On the screen, a man and a woman were in a boat, and it looked like a storm was brewing. When the boat capsized, the four of them decided to leave and check out the rest of the library, and Worthington came with them.

"When I'm finished here, I'll be reading in the atrium," he whispered. "Come find me when you're done with Mr. Abelman."

They said they would. As they walked away, Jupiter said, "Just as I hoped. I brought the DVD of *Dawn Over Petrograd* with me, and since there aren't very many people watching *Sunrise,* perhaps we can persuade Mr. Abelman to arrange for us to screen it in the screening room. I have the feeling it might be easier to find its hidden clues if we could see it on a big screen."

"What a great idea!" Mallory said. Bob agreed − though if it happened, he felt a little sorry for Worthington, since the movie was probably two hours long.

Soon, they were in the library itself.

"This is quite a collection," Mallory said, shading her eyes and looking up at the two stories above her.

"It really seems so," Bob said. Out of what he thought was a kind of professional courtesy, he walked up to the Circulation Desk. A woman whose name tag announced her as Anita Rodriguez approached him.

"Can I help you?" she asked in a friendly way.

"Hi," Bob said. "I'm Bob Andrews, and I work part-time at the Rocky Beach Library." By this time he'd been joined by Jupiter, Mallory, and Pete. "Could you tell us about this library?" he asked.

"Well, we opened about thirty years

ago," Ms. Rodriguez said. "We've done our best to put together as complete a record of film as we can." She turned and gestured behind her. "Here in the open stacks are the things people want most often — books about movie stars and movies, about directors and other people who worked in film, and of course about film history. We also have over twenty thousand DVDs of films that we loan out."

She pointed up at the two floors above her. "Those stacks are restricted," she said. "If you want something, one of the librarians will bring it to you, and you can examine it or work with it in one of the research rooms. But nothing up there leaves the library. The older and rarer films are up there, including many that have been digitally re-mastered just for us. That's also where we keep the most valuable books, and all the research material — the manuscripts and screenplays and shooting scripts, letters and papers of people in the industry."

"What about those elevators?" Jupiter asked. "It looks like anyone could use them."

"Anyone could," Ms. Rodriguez said. "But they don't."

"This is terrific," Mallory said. "We're lucky to have access to something like this."

Ms. Rodriguez looked pleased. "That's nice of you to say," she said. "We think it's pretty special. And downstairs in the basement we have thousands of old movie posters and odd items of interest. One of Charlie Chaplin's canes, for example, and a facsimile of Rosebud."

When Pete looked puzzled, Ms. Rodriguez said, "The sled from *Citizen Kane.*" Pete still looked puzzled.

"Do you have anything from *Time Twist?*" he asked. "Our friend – "

Jupiter bumped his elbow and Pete stopped talking.

Ms. Rodriguez smiled. "Nothing yet," she said. "But the new one hasn't even opened."

"That's right!" Pete said, "We're – "

Jupiter shook his head.

"Thanks very much," Bob said. "We'll let you get back to your work."

"Just one thing," Jupiter said. "We're actually here to meet Mr. Jason Abelman. Would you have a way of contacting him to see if he's able to see us now?"

"Certainly," Ms. Rodriguez said. "Come this way."

Pete and Jupiter followed, but as Bob

turned to go after them, he suddenly noticed, off to the right, a row of varnished oak cupboards, each one with serried ranks of small drawers – a card catalogue, from the days before online public access catalogues!

Each of the drawers was filled with index-card sized slips of paper, one for each book or other item in the library's collection. Each had a hole punched in the middle bottom, and a metal rod held all the cards in place.

"Look at that!" Bob said to Mallory, pointing. "An old card catalogue!"

All Bob's life, he'd been able to use a computer to look up books, but he'd often used the original card catalogue in the Rocky Beach library – which had kept the old system in place until about three years ago.

It was low-tech, but there was something dignified and comfortingly intimate about it; each card had been touched by thousands of human hands and bore the marks in pencil and pen that librarians and others had made on the pre-printed cards.

The card catalogues showed quite dramatically the interaction between the library's patrons and the library's holdings. With an online catalogue, you might as well have been the very first person in the world to ever be interested in a particular book.

"I've never seen one," Mallory said. "The library I used in Scotland had gone digital by the time I started taking out books."

"Miss Bennett insisted on keeping ours until about three years ago," Bob said. "But now, even that one's gone. I bet this library kept theirs as an exhibit. After all, this is sort of a museum, too."

"Let's go look at it," Mallory said. Bob looked up to see Pete and Jupiter standing at the end of the hall leading to the offices. Evidently Ms. Rodriguez had walked down to see if Mr. Abelman was available. He thought he and Mallory had time to see the card catalogue.

Right off, Bob was struck by a printed notice that read, under the word WARNING, "This catalogue has not been updated since 1999."

"That's years before any of us were born!" Bob said.

Mallory was busy reading down the alphabetical listing of what was in each drawer. Bob watched as she pulled out the drawer labeled FOA – FUN and started rifling through the cards at the back of the file. She was searching for FORD, EDISON he thought.

"Nothing," she said.

"That's not surprising," Bob said. "You wouldn't expect to find his novels in a library like this."

He pulled out a drawer quite close to the one Mallory had looked in.

"FEB – FON. FEDOROV, VADIM. Look!"

There were about two dozen cards, each one listing a screenplay Vadim had written before he was blacklisted. "Wow!" Bob said. "Multiple shooting scripts for a bunch of his movies. With handwritten annotations."

"I guess people who worked on the films donated their copies to the library," Mallory said.

"If you were really interested in researching how a movie changed as it was being written and shot, this would be the place to do your work," Bob said.

He flipped to the end of Vadim's entries and found FEDOROV, YURI. "They even have LPs of some of Ivan's father's soundtracks."

"If we do our job properly," Mallory said, "maybe they'll have a card for FEDOROV, IVAN before too long. Or not a card, but an entry in their online catalogue."

Bob smiled in agreement. Idly, he kept

flipping through cards, pausing randomly at
FILCHER, FJOSNE, FLANAGAN. He stopped
when he came to FODEROV, V. He was struck
instantly by how similar the name was to Fedorov. It was amazing how the transposition of
two vowels changed things – two people, whose
last name was spelled just a little bit differently.

He looked carefully at the card. Under
the author's name he saw some very strange
words. He blinked a few times, as though the
unfamiliar letters might resolve and communicate something to him, but they stayed fixed.
Unless he was mistaken, those were Cyrillic letters – the kinds of letters they used in Russia.
There seemed to be no translation. A handwritten note at the bottom of the card said it was a
gift to the museum.

All of a sudden Jupiter and Pete had
joined them. "Let's go," Pete said. "Mr. Abelman's ready." Bob slid the drawer shut and followed Jupiter, who was already walking away.
He seemed to know where he was going.

They were about to head down the hallway to the left of the screening room when a
security guard stopped them. He was dressed
in blue, with a black belt and black boots; he
had big sideburns and squinty eyes.

"Not so fast," he said. "Where do you

think you're going? Unauthorized personnel aren't allowed down there."

"We have an appointment with Mr. Jason Abelman," Jupiter said calmly. "He's expecting us."

Without saying anything, the man stepped aside, still glowering – but, as Pete walked past him, he shoved him slightly. Pete bristled, but walked on.

Mr. Abelman had a corner office, with windows on two sides. The fabric blinds had been pulled against the sun's glare, but the room was suffused with warm light. Bob thought the place was a happy mess – the office of someone who liked what he did. The desk was crowded with papers and folders. Teetering piles of books were stacked on the floor. But a sofa and several easy chairs were clear, and soon they were all seated comfortably. All except Pete, who was still seething from their run-in with the guard.

"So how do you like our library?" Mr. Abelman asked. His tweed sports jacket hung on the back of his chair. He was wearing a pastel blue shirt and a yellow bow tie, but his eyes and forehead looked a lot like Cassandra's.

"It's great, except for some jerk guard

we just ran into," Pete said.

"Yes," Mr. Abelman said. "The director should talk to him. He's a nasty piece of work. He doesn't like working here – or anywhere! – but he got the job because of Congressman Clark."

"Douglas Clark?" Jupiter asked.

"Yes," Mr. Abelman said. "The father of the little monster who's giving my son-in-law a headache. Most of our funding comes from foundations and private donations, but we recently received a grant from the federal government, courtesy of Clark, and that guard seems to have come with it."

"Why is he here?" Mallory asked. "You don't find security guards at most libraries."

"I don't really know," Mr. Abelman said. "He must have been a bouncer in a former life. He seems to want to throw most patrons out on their ears. He'd be better off as a guard in a gulag than a library. There's nothing worse than people ending up in the wrong line of work! But Cassandra tells me the four of you are well-suited for investigating. How did you get started?"

Jupiter immediately warmed to the task, and Bob was afraid they were in for a long recital, but Jupiter surprised him by keeping the explanation short. He then asked if Mr. Abelman had records of the interviews he had conducted with Ivan's father, Yuri, before his death.

"Yes, indeed," Mr. Abelman said. He rose from his desk and went to a filing cabinet from which he extracted a thick folder. After sorting through it, he returned with a sheaf of papers.

"Who should I give these to?" he asked. "They're transcriptions of the interviews. I've got extra copies, so you can have them, if you want."

"Thank you," Jupiter said. "You should give them to Bob. He's Records and Research."

"And you're organized too!" Mr. Abelman said, handing the papers to Bob. He gestured at his desk and floor. "I could learn a thing or two from the four of you," he said, as he sat back down in his swivel chair. "The fact is, I could have simply sent you PDFs of the transcripts without you having to come all the way to Boxwood. Not that I'm not glad to meet you, of course," he said politely.

"We're glad to be here," said Jupiter. "And we're hoping you might be able to help us get permission to watch *Dawn Over Petrograd* in the screening room. Last night, when we were at Ivan and Cassandra's, they lent us a copy and told us the story about how Fyodor supposedly wove clues into the movie which would let an attentive viewer know that he disapproved of the movie's treatment of the Russian Revolution."

"That's right!" Mr. Abelman exclaimed. "And I'm embarrassed to admit that, although I've seen the film, I wasn't able to find any clues at all. I'm sure I could help you get permission – though not today. The head librarian, Ms. Rodriguez, has a very strict rule about needing at least 24 hours' notice to reserve the room for a private screening. When I leave, I'll ask her if you can reserve it for later in the week. Unfortunately, we're closed tomorrow."

"That would be great," Jupiter said.

They spent another fifteen or twenty minutes with Mr. Abelman, but although he did a lot of very funny imitations of supposedly Russian accents in a lot of American movies, he kept saying that everything he could tell them about his interviews with Yuri would be in the transcripts, and at last Jupiter decided that it was time to leave.

As they walked down the hall toward the atrium, Bob was astounded to see Tracey

Clark talking to the surly guard who'd hassled Pete earlier. She had what looked like a bunch of CDs in her hand, and she was gesturing with them. Bob hadn't been formally introduced to her, but he'd seen her the previous night at the party and he had no doubt that this was her. Mallory pulled Pete and Bob aside.

"Remember the cover story," she said, "if we talk to her."

Bob could hardly have forgotten it, but Tracey was so involved in her conversation that she didn't notice them as they walked past her into the atrium. He assumed that Tracey and the guard knew each other through Tracey's father and were talking about him. So he was puzzled when he caught a fragment of their conversation.

"So I can't go up there?" Tracey said.

The guard shook his head. "Restricted access," he said. "Only research librarians. But the place is closed on Wednesdays, and I'm on duty."

"Tomorrow?" Tracey said.

He heard nothing more as they got further away, but just then Tracey turned and caught sight of Mallory and Jupiter. She looked surprised, but not displeased, and she came right over. "Hello, again," she said. "What are you doing here?"

"More research for our paper," Mallory said smoothly. "These are the two other members of our group – Bob Andrews and Pete Crenshaw."

"Pleased to meet you," Bob said.

"I'm just here a quick minute," Tracey said. "I'm picking up some movies to use as research for my novel. Which I'm happy to say is almost finished! In fact, I'm bringing one of the concluding chapters to my writing group when we meet tomorrow afternoon."

"Congratulations," Mallory said – whether sincerely or insincerely Bob couldn't really tell. "I wish I could read it!"

"Well, you can," Tracey said, "if you want. Why don't you join us tomorrow? I'd love to have you come as my guest. We meet each week at a different member's house, and tomorrow we're meeting at mine. It'll be sort of a party to celebrate my finishing. My brother and a cousin will be grilling hamburgers and veggie burgers. Here, let me give you my address and phone number." She took a pen and a notepad from her purse, wrote on it, and handed the paper to Mallory.

"Would the rest of you like to come as

well?" Tracey asked. "I'm sure you could gather more information for your paper."

"Thank you," Jupiter said. "That's very kind of you. But the rest of us have plans."

"Come if you change your mind," Tracey said. "There'll be plenty to eat. We start at 4:00 and usually break by 7:00. So I'll see you?" She looked inquiringly at Mallory.

"I really don't know yet," Mallory said. "But I'll think about it. I appreciate the invitation."

"Bye," Tracey said, as she turned to leave.

They watched her walk across the atrium, through the tall doors, and down the granite steps toward the parking lot.

"She doesn't seem so bad," Pete said.

"Which doesn't mean that she isn't," said Jupiter. "I found her behavior quite suspicious yesterday evening. And just now, when she tilted her hand to write down the information for Mallory, I could see that the top DVD on her pile was *Dawn over Petrograd*."

"Whoa!" Pete said. "That's weird."

Yes, Bob thought. My sentiments exactly. But just as he was about to say something else, he saw Worthington approaching them with a familiar-looking man at his side.

As Worthington waved, the man did, too, and
although it still took Bob a moment to recognize him, he was in no doubt when Pete said
excitedly, "It's Per Jorgensen!"

8

Some Truly Curious Clues

It was! Pete thought. And most amazing of all, as Pete was recognizing *him*, *he* was recognizing Pete!

"Is that my friend Pete Crenshaw?" he called out, as he strolled down the hall. They were hardly friends, Pete thought, but Pete's father, who was a construction manager and set supervisor in film, had worked on *The Seventh Messenger* – the movie for which Per Jorgensen had been nominated for the Oscar.

Since his father had gotten to know Mr. Jorgensen a little, when The Three Investigators had needed information about why a painting he'd donated to the Center For Falconry and Fencing might have been stolen, Pete had asked his father if he could call Mr. Jorgensen and set up a meeting with him.

The resulting investigation had been good for the Center For Falconry and Fencing, The Three Investigators, and for Pete. Of course, the reason Per Jorgensen recognized him right away was probably because Worthington had already told him The Three Investigators were in the library. But even so, Pete was really flattered and excited – so excited that the first thing that emerged from his mouth was, "I still have that piece of driftwood you gave me – though I never carved it into a falcon!"

Per Jorgensen laughed. "I'm glad you liked it, anyway," he said. He was tall and slender but also very rugged-looking. His gray eyes were intense and his high cheekbones and square stubbled chin made him look like the movie star he was.

"I do!" Pete blurted out. "But what are you doing *here*? I mean, if you don't mind my asking."

Per Jorgensen laughed again. "Not at all," he said. "I've been wanting to direct a film for a long time now, and I've been offered a script set in the time of the Viking empire. I'm here to do some research about other Viking movies. As for what you and your friends are doing here, I'm betting it has to do with a case."

"You're right!" Pete said. "A case involving a movie you're in!"

"Really?" said Per Jorgensen. "What movie is that?"

Pete was feeling so star-struck that, at

the moment, he couldn't remember the name of the movie, but luckily, Mallory and Jupiter did. Almost at the same time, they said, *"The Golden Age"* – after which Jupiter explained that their client was Ivan Fedorov, and that a one-time high school classmate had accused him of having plagiarized the song he'd written for the movie.

"Ivan tells us that the director may pull the song completely if there's a chance the accuser could get an injunction to prevent the movie's release," Jupiter said.

"Oh, no," Per Jorgensen said. "That sounds serious. The film industry can be quite cutthroat. But Ivan Fedorov is very talented, and surely there's nothing to the accusation. But what does the Film History Library have to do with this?"

"Nothing, really," Pete started to say, but Jupiter interrupted.

"We're not sure," he said. "But we've learned that Ivan's great-grandfather, Fyodor Fedorov, did something quite interesting when he was in a 1937 film called *Dawn Over Petrograd*. He was playing a Bolshevik during the Russian Revolution, and it seems he may have demonstrated his disdain for the way the Revolution was being depicted by the director by engaging in some subversive actions. I was hoping we could use the screening room of the library to see if we could determine what those actions were, but we weren't able to get permission to screen the film today."

Just then, Ms. Rodriguez, who had been walking from the Circulation Desk to one of the offices along Mr. Abelman's corridor noticed Per Jorgensen. Her face lit up, and she blushed. As a blusher himself from way back, Pete felt sorry for her. She clearly had a crush on Per, Pete thought.

"Mr. Jorgensen!" she said brightly. "How nice to see you again! I'm so excited about everything I've heard about *The Golden Age*! I read that you play one of Catherine the Great's lovers!" She blushed even more brightly when she said this.

Since all of The Three Investigators' dealings with Per Jorgensen the summer before had occurred at his house on the ocean, this was the first time Pete had ever seen the effect he had on women, and he couldn't help but feel both sorry for him and envious at the same time.

"A minor one," Per Jorgensen said.

"Well, I'm sure you're wonderful," said Ms. Rodriguez. "Is there anything in particular

I can help you with today?"

"I don't think so," Per Jorgensen said. "But perhaps you could help my young friends here. They have an old classic movie they'd like to screen – a film from 1937, starring Fyodor Fedorov – and they think they'll have to come back some other day to do it. Is that true?"

His voice was a throaty sort of rumble that Pete felt would have melted the heart of even a woman who *didn't* have a crush on him. Plus that *accent*!

"They want to see a film in the screening room?" said Ms. Rodriguez. "And they're friends of yours? Well, I'll have to check to make sure that it's empty, but if it is, I don't see why they couldn't use it." She turned and vanished into the auditorium. When she came back, she was smiling.

"There's no one using it now," she said. "They can just go right on in."

"How excellent," said Per, smiling. "Thank you very much."

At this, Ms. Rodriguez bobbed and almost did a curtsy, then turned toward the office she'd been headed for to begin with. Pete, Bob, Mallory and Jupiter all thanked Per profusely.

Before he left to head toward the stacks, Per said to all of them – apparently quite sincerely – "Please let me know if there's anything else I can do – either for you or for Ivan Fedorov. In fact, please call me when you get a little further along in the case. What you've told me has made me quite angry. You should still have my phone number."

"We do," Bob said – and after Per Jorgensen had disappeared, he turned to Worthington. "Is this O.K. with you?" he asked. "We didn't expect to be here as long as this, already, and if we see the whole film, we may be here another two hours. Do you want us to find another way home?"

"As a matter of fact," Worthington said, "It would be fun to see the film with you. And since I have a bit of experience as an actor, maybe I can even be of some help in noticing anything odd."

Soon, they were all sitting in luxurious seats, in a luxurious row. Ms. Rodriguez had given Jupiter an elaborate device that controlled the DVD projecting the film on the big screen and showed him how to use it.

"Everyone ready?" Jupiter asked.

Pete sure was.

The movie opened with a shot of a thoroughbred racehorse running – the icon of the studio that had made the movie – and then the credits rolled.

Worthington said, "In this era, the credits were usually at the beginning of a film."

Among the listed actors, Pete didn't recognize any names, except for "Fyodor Fedorov" in prominent letters.

"What should we be looking for?" Bob asked.

"Props," Jupiter said. "Something Fyodor Fedorov handles, or something used to dress the sets. I don't think it could be anything in the dialogue, action, or stage sets themselves; those would all be out of Fyodor's control. It has to be something small − something he could introduce into the movie without anyone noticing."

Everyone nodded as the movie began. Pete was impressed by the establishing shots of a majestic city that he assumed was standing in for the real St. Petersburg. The plot started slowly, but soon the hero and heroine appeared, and not long after, the other major characters − among them Andreev Popov, the character played by Fyodor Fedorov.

"There he is," Pete said, pointing. But soon he was dismayed to discover that the movie was *filled* with props − too many to keep track of. Rifles and machine guns, parasols, lead pipes, lanterns, knapsacks, food and drink, canes and crutches – all of it came and went with dizzying speed. Though Pete tried as hard as he could to concentrate, he kept feeling that things were escaping him, and in very short order, he gave up and just sank into the story of the film.

But just as Pete was thinking what a commanding figure Fyodor Fedorov cut, Jupiter suddenly froze the film in its tracks.

"Wait!" Pete said. "We're getting to an exciting part!"

Jupiter ignored him. He was staring at a close-up of Andreev Popov dressed elaborately, wearing a large and distinguished-looking medal on his chest – a black enamel cross, with a gold double-headed eagle appearing in the four spaces between the arms of the cross. No one said anything as Jupiter studied it. Finally, he turned to Bob, who had brought his laptop into the screening room with him.

"Bob, could you research Russian medals?" Jupiter said.

"Sure, Jupe," Bob said, opening his laptop. "What do you want me to look for?"

"Try something like 'Awards of Russia,'" Jupiter answered.

"I've got a choice between Awards of the

Russian Federation and Awards of the Russian Empire," he said.

"Empire," Jupiter said decisively.

"Can we just watch the movie?" Pete said plaintively.

"In a minute," Jupiter said.

"Here it is," Bob said. He handed the laptop to Jupiter. "As far as I can see," he said, "Fyodor Fedorov is wearing the Imperial Order of St. Ivan – an award given by the Czar for meritorious service in the arts. It could be just a coincidence, but I don't think so."

"I don't think so, either," said Jupiter. "The character has nothing to do with the theater, but we know that Fyodor Fedorov was awarded a medal by the czar for his work there. Even if that medal isn't the one he got from the czar, it's a medal from Imperial Russia, and nothing a Bolshevik would have worn."

Pete was impressed by this piece of deduction, but he hoped that the movie could just proceed now. However, the next clue came fifteen minutes later, in the form of a bunch of posters on a kiosk in a train station. Jupiter stopped the film again and studied them. After his success with the medal, Pete was willing to grant him a little more leeway, and in fact had become reinvolved in the hunt for clues himself.

Several times he thought maybe he'd seen something, but Jupiter hadn't stopped the film.

The posters were anachronistically in English, but then the film was for an English audience, Pete thought. Most of them featured stylized silhouettes of figures, chins raised, staring into a bright and glorious future. They were emblazoned with language about the Peoples' Waterworks and the Commune's Electricity — announcing the new world order the Communists were ushering in.

But among them was one poster that seemed to have been left behind from a previous era. It looked very out-of-place surrounded by its comrades. It dated from the days before the revolution and prominently featured a realistic picture of a public park with people picnicking beside a river and parading with parasols. Some were reading books, others were playing the violin, or dangling their feet in the river. A gaggle of children played nearby.

What had drawn Jupiter's attention to the poster — which might have entirely escaped Pete's notice — was the fact that Andreev Popov was pounding on it with his fist, while he gave an impassioned speech about the workers' council and the newly-controlled waterworks. It would clearly have made sense if he'd been thumping the waterworks poster. But instead he was pounding on the picture of people at leisure, enjoying themselves.

Jupiter rewound the film to the beginning of the scene and let it run again.

"And comrades, let us never forget," Fyodor Fedorov said as he pounded on the poster of the picnickers, "that for all the pain and suffering the Czarist regime inflicted on our country, the heart of Mother Russia is, and always will be, honest people like these."

Jupiter paused the film again. "See?" he said. "Would a Bolshevik have been going on about the fact that the Russian middle class was the heart of the country?"

"I don't think that means too much," Pete said. "He could just have hit the wrong poster."

But Jupiter shook his head. "That poster should never have been on the set to begin with, if the set dressers had been properly doing their jobs. I would guess it was surreptitiously pasted there by Fedorov's co-conspirator."

The third clue was definitive, as far as Jupiter was concerned. The scene took place in a library where a bunch of Bolsheviks were having a meeting about how best to bring education to the masses. Fedorov's character stood pompously and reached for a book on one of the shelves.

As he pulled it down, he said, "I cannot wait until every child of the motherland is able to lift a book like this from the shelf and read it." He brandished the book, gesturing with its spine toward the camera.

Swiftly Jupiter paused the film. Pete could see the title clearly – though strangely it wasn't in English letters but in the Russian letters Pete thought were called Cyrillic.

Below the title was a hammer and sickle in bright red.

Even Pete got a tingly feeling as he stared at the book. Nothing else in the film had been in Cyrillic letters – no street sign, or business placard, no poster or newspaper headline. The dialogue had been in English, not Russian. So why this? he wondered.

Jupiter turned to Bob. "Could you copy down those letters carefully on a piece of paper so that we can look them up?" he said.

"Sure, Jupe," Bob said. It seemed to take forever as he squinted at the screen and then made marks on a piece of paper. More than once he erased an unfamiliar letter and tried again.

"Got it!" Bob finally said when he was

done.

Jupiter looked at Bob who was staring down at the words he'd copied. He had an odd expression on his face. "What is it?" Jupiter asked.

"I can't be sure," Bob said. "I don't know the Cyrillic alphabet at all. But I have to say that what I just copied down looks an awful lot like the words I just found on a file in the old card catalogue." He looked up doubtfully. "I'm sure I'm wrong," he said.

"What library card?" Jupiter asked intently. The hair on the back of Pete's neck stood up. They were onto something.

Jupiter turned the movie off entirely.

"There's an old-style physical card catalogue at the Circulation Desk. You saw Mallory and me in front of it," Bob said.

"Yes," said Jupiter, "but I didn't know what you were doing."

"Mallory and I were looking up Edison Ford and Vadim Fedorov, and I came across a card for someone named V. Foderov – just like Fedorov, but with the first two vowels reversed. The library owns a manuscript by him, but the title was in Cyrillic."

Jupiter leaned forward in his excitement. "The title wasn't translated into English?"

"No," Bob said.

"Was there anything else on the card?"

"Someone had written on it that the manuscript was a gift of some woman. I can't remember the name. Can you, Mallory?"

Mallory shook her head.

"Try to remember," Jupiter said.

Bob winced. "I think the first name was Helene, or something. And the last name was sort of like Oreos. I don't know. The only real way to find out would be to go back and look."

"I think we're going to have to do that before we leave," Jupiter said, "but in the meantime, is there any way you can find out what the title says in English?"

"I can try," Bob said. "Let's see if there's a way to type Cyrillic letters using an English keyboard." He searched for a minute, hit EN-TER, and said, "Here it is. It's a site called Typeit. There's a virtual keyboard with Cyrillic letters. I can just click letter by letter, matching what I wrote down with the keyboard."

"That's great," Jupiter said.

"Hold on," Bob said. "This'll give hunt-and-peck a whole new meaning. Just leave me alone while I do this."

Pete tried to be patient as Bob set to work. Laboriously, he went back and forth between the letters he'd written down and the virtual keyboard on his laptop. Slowly the letters appeared on-screen – the title of the book Fedorov had been holding.

At last Bob was finished. "Now all I have to do is find a Russian-to-English translator," he said. He choose a site called Yandex Translate.

He copied and pasted the transliteration into the search box, and instantly English words appeared in the opposite box.

A thrill ran up Pete's spine.

INTEMPERATE IMPERIUM, it read.

"What a weird title," Bob said. "I think "imperium" is just another word for "empire" – and I can see why that word, in Russian, might translate to the fancier version of the word in English. But "intemperate" seems a little weird."

"Why don't you see if there are any synonyms you like better?" Jupiter said.

Bob typed for a minute on his laptop. "It could mean 'extreme' or 'immoderate.' Or even 'uncontrolled' or 'unbridled' or 'uninhibited.'"

But Jupiter already seemed triumphant. "Whatever the first Russian word actually is, the meaning seems clear," he said. "Fyodor Fedorov brandished that title like a sword.

Over the hammer and sickle – the sign of the Communist party – the words were accusing the Soviets of the very thing they had supposedly fought against – using unrestrained power against the Russian people."

Even Pete felt excited about the find.

"If we're not going to see the rest of the movie," he said, "then I think we should go find that card in the card catalogue. Bob can take the page with the Russian letters and compare it to the Russian letters on the card. If they really are the same letters, then maybe – well – maybe – " He stopped, realizing that he didn't really know what he wanted to say.

"Maybe someone else cracked the code of the movie," said Mallory. "Maybe someone wrote a paper, or a dissertation or something, about Fyodor Fedorov and what he did in *Dawn Over Petrograd*. Maybe the woman whose name Bob and I can't remember – the one who donated whatever it was to the library – was actually a writer who had written about the movie and who wanted her work to have a permanent home."

"We'll know more when we find the card," Jupiter said. "Let's go."

He picked up the device Ms. Rodriguez had given him and retrieved the DVD while

Bob gathered up his stuff and Worthington checked to make sure that no one had forgotten anything. They left the auditorium, and then they all – except Worthington – made their way back to the Circulation Desk. Jupiter talked to Ms. Rodriguez while Bob and Mallory opened the appropriate drawer.

Pete watched as first Mallory and then Bob rifled through the cards, first locating Fedorov, and then trying to find Foderov. They were talking together as they bent over the open drawer, and although Pete couldn't exactly understand what the hold-up was, it seemed clear that they were having trouble finding the card they were looking for again. They stopped and started over, then stopped and started over again.

At last, the two of them joined Pete and Jupiter. Bob, in particular, looked disturbed. "I can't find it," he said. "*We* can't find it. We both saw it and now it's gone. I really can't believe it. I'd think I was going crazy if Mallory hadn't seen it, too."

"I did, though," said Mallory. "Someone must have ripped it out of the drawer after we left. The cards are just attached through punch holes. It wouldn't be hard to rip one out and put it in your pocket."

"But who would have done that?" said Pete. "And why?"

"The *why* answers itself," said Jupiter. "Because the card is an important clue to something the person who took it doesn't want us to know. As for who would have done that, the better question is who could have. There haven't been all that many people here since we arrived. And only one of those people was also carrying a copy of *Dawn Over Petrograd.* Tracey Clark!"

9

Another Russian Émigré

Jupiter knew he really shouldn't feel triumphant at having almost certainly been proved right in his instinct about Tracey Clark, but he really couldn't help it – especially after he had also figured out what might prove a truly important clue in the movie Fyodor Fedorov had won his Oscar for.

He felt very grateful to Per Jorgensen – and also to Per Jorgensen's apparently irresistible appeal to women – for having arranged with Ms. Rodriguez for The Three Investigators to use the screening room. If they hadn't been able to see the movie here, they wouldn't have been able to find out so swiftly that the card Bob and Mallory had discovered in the card catalogue was now gone – and he therefore wouldn't have had such swift validation of his instinct that Tracey Clark was a bad one, just like her brother.

Until he and the others put together the whole story of what was really going on – until they solved the case – he would have no real reason to feel triumphant, of course. But since up until now he'd been feeling a little guilty about taking the day off from Ivan's more pressing – or at least more immediate – problem, at least he didn't feel guilty any more.

In fact, as they all left the library and piled into the Flex for the ride back to Rocky Beach, he felt very organized and energized. Tomorrow, the four of them would devote all their time and attention to the underlying case. It would be Wednesday and the American Film History Library was closed all day on Wednesdays.

Still, even if it had been open, at the moment there really was nothing else The Three Investigators needed to do there, and once they arrived back at the Salvage Yard, Jupiter – remembering the effect Per Jorgensen had had on Ms. Rodriguez – suddenly had the thought that maybe Per could prove helpful in any interviews Bob was able to arrange with Colton and Ivan's classmates. If he was correct in believing that those classmates might not respond to fourteen-year-old questioners in quite the way that Ivan and Cassandra hoped, then maybe they'd be more forthcoming if they were questioned by a famous movie star.

He broached this idea to the others. "There's no way *anyone* would refuse to talk with Per Jorgensen!" Bob said, so Jupiter asked Pete if he wanted to call Per that evening when he got home to ask if he would help. If he could, then Bob should go with Pete and Per to keep the interviews organized − and maybe even to tape them.

As for him and Mallory, he thought that tomorrow they should read through the transcripts of Jason Abelman's interview with Ivan's father to see if they could find anything interesting or suggestive, and maybe also go back to see Mrs. Vasiliev to see if she knew anything about Yuri or Vadim she hadn't mentioned yet.

Needless to say, Pete was practically delirious at the thought that he and Bob might be spending tomorrow morning interviewing a bunch of Ivan's old classmates in the company of Per Jorgensen − and Bob didn't seem all that unhappy about the idea, either.

Jupiter suggested that as soon as they knew whether Per Jorgensen was willing to help, Bob should send an e-mail to the seven people he had contact information for, saying that Per Jorgensen and their old classmate Ivan Fedorov had been working on a movie together and that Per and The Three Investigators would like to talk to them about a graduation party they'd been to.

He should ask if they'd all be willing to meet on the grounds of the high school itself; it would be a lot more efficient to do the interviews one after another, and it would take up a lot less of Per's time if he didn't have to drive all over Los Angeles.

With that arranged, the four of them split up and headed to their homes for dinner and their various tasks. To Jupiter's pleasure, Pete called him to say that Per Jorgensen had said yes, and when the seven classmates learned about his involvement, they were all willing, too. More than willing, from what Bob said when he called to report. That night, Jupiter went to bed with a sense of accomplishment that let him sleep very well. The next morning, Mallory would come to the Salvage Yard to meet him. Then they'd bike to the Rocky Beach Library to start the day by reading the transcripts of Jason Abelman's interviews with Yuri Fedorov.

Unfortunately, in the morning, things did not go precisely as planned. Although Per had arranged to pick up Bob and Pete at their houses a little later in the morning, Bob and Pete suddenly showed up on their bikes because Bob had left a bunch of his notes on the desk in Headquarters, and he had to pick them up to take them with him.

Aunt Mathilda and Uncle Titus came out to talk to the four of them, and when Uncle Titus asked what case The Three Investigators were working on now, Pete started to explain. He managed to mention that the day before they'd all seen a movie in the screening room at the American Film History Library. Aunt Mathilda exclaimed, "You watched a movie? In the middle of the day?"

"Just for a case," said Bob. "We're trying to help a man named Ivan Fedorov, and the movie stars his great-grandfather."

"I don't see the connection," Aunt Mathilda said, "but if you say so."

"Fedorov," Uncle Titus murmured. He frowned. "Is that – ?"

"Russian," Jupiter said. "And the movie's about the Russian Revolution."

"Well, Jupiter," Uncle Titus said. "A movie about Bolshies, in the middle of the day." He sighed and shook his head in mock disappointment, but as Mallory pulled up on her bike, his eyes gleamed. Jupiter could see what was coming. So could his friends.

"In order to make up for such a lazy way of working, I'm afraid you'll have to – "

He paused.

"Solve. This. Puzzle," Pete, Bob, and Mallory said in unison.

Uncle Titus smiled benignly. "It's not a puzzle really – more of a conundrum. I'll make it Russian-themed in honor of your case. Let's see." He squinted, looked up at the sky, and rubbed his hand over his chin. "This, of course, happened before the Revolution." He cleared his throat.

"There was this Russian landowner, and he had two sons. He was nearing the end of his days, and he could only leave his holdings to one of them."

"The older one?" Jupiter asked.

"That's what you'd think," Uncle Titus said, lifting a finger. "But this was an enlightened landowner, and he wanted to give his younger son a chance. So he devised a test. 'We will have a race,' he said. 'Each of you will ride your favorite reindeer, and whichever reindeer crosses the finish line second will secure the estate for its owner.'"

"Crosses the finish line *second?*" Pete said.

"Second," Uncle Titus affirmed. "So the brothers got on their reindeer and started walking toward the finish line. But whenever one or the other got close, he drew back. They wandered aimlessly for days, doing anything they could to avoid the finish line, until they were almost dead from hunger and thirst. Finally they came upon a wise man with a long white beard, wearing a hair shirt and sitting in a tree."

Jupiter could see Uncle Titus was really warming to his tale, but he wished he'd hurry up. They all had tasks to do today, and Bob and Pete were on an actual schedule.

"They got down from their reindeer and lay on the ground, totally spent. The wise man looked at them and took pity. 'What can I do for you?' he said, and the brothers asked him for advice. No sooner had the wise man spoken than the brothers leaped on the reindeer and made a mad dash for the finish line, riding as fast as they could."

"This is a weird story," Pete said.

"So," Uncle Titus said, fixing Jupiter with his eyes. "What did the wise men tell the brothers?" He looked very pleased with himself, Jupiter thought.

Without missing a beat, Jupiter said, in a cool steady voice, "He told them to switch reindeer."

"Aha!" Uncle Titus said, leaping around on the gravel. "You never disappoint, my boy."

"Wait," Bob said. "I don't get it."

"Me neither," said Pete.

"It has to do with the reindeer," Mallory explained. "After they switched reindeer, they were riding one another's, so they each wanted to be first across the finish line so that their *actual* reindeer would be second."

"Exactly," Uncle Titus said. "Good for you, Mallory."

Yes, indeed, Jupiter thought.

"So we'll be going now," he said, moving toward his bike.

Soon, he and Mallory were pulling up to the Rocky Beach library and locking up their bikes. Not long after, they were sitting side by side with the transcripts Jason Abelman had given them on the table before them.

But before they started reading, Mallory suddenly said, "I've been thinking about Tracey Clark's invitation to go to the writers' group meeting she's having at her house tonight. The whole idea of a writers' group makes me sick, but when you said what you said about her being the only one who could really have taken that card from the card catalogue, I started thinking maybe I should go. It would give me a chance to check out her house and see if I could find anything relevant to the case."

Jupiter decided not to ask Mallory why

the idea of a writers' group made her sick. He just said, "That's true. Where does she live again?"

"Not far from Cassandra and Ivan," Mallory said. "And I bet I could get Cassandra to pick me up and drive me there. Wait. Let me see what her house looks like."

She opened her laptop and got on a real estate site called Zillow, where she got indirect confirmation that Tracey had bought her house about two years ago. A little more research led to the information that the house had originally belonged to a man named Ivan Ivanovich.

"That's pretty weird," Mallory said. "A lot weirder than your uncle's story about the reindeer. Though Ivan is a pretty common Russian name, it's still strange to have another Ivan pop up out of nowhere like that – "

"Maybe you should go," Jupiter said. "But for now, let's read these transcripts." As they read, they conferred with one another, and between them they were able to put together a fairly solid story – and also an interesting one.

As they already knew, Vadim Fedorov, after he was blacklisted, had essentially changed his identity. He'd become Edison Ford. He'd rarely given interviews, but when he had, he'd never talked about his parents Fyodor or Marinka, or Russia – or even about his screenplays. Nevertheless, he had gotten involved with, and financially supported, an organization that helped Russian émigrés get settled in California.

After all, he knew firsthand how hard things had been for his mother and father, and there were lots of émigrés. In the interview, Yuri confirmed that between the time his father was blacklisted and the time the Soviet Union fell, a quarter of a million Soviet Jews had been allowed to immigrate to the United States, and many of them came to California.

According to Yuri's story, Fyodor's mother had been Jewish, so that meant he was technically Jewish. But Marinka had been Russian Orthodox. Since Jewishness was matrilineal, Vadim wasn't Jewish, nor were Yuri nor Ivan. Anyway, the point was that most everyone in Hollywood thought of Fyodor as a White Russian, including his own grandson, Yuri – who was very surprised when his father Vadim did what he did to help Soviet Jews who had come to America.

Also according to Yuri's story, his father had become great friends with one of them – a younger woman, who Yuri had wanted to date.

But she wasn't interested in him. She was really only interested in Vadim.

In the transcript, the relevant section read as follows:

"You said your father became close to a young Jewish woman from Novoskibirsk," Mr. Abelman had said.

"Yes," Yuri Fedorov had said. *"He worked with several people, helping them settle in, getting them jobs or apartments. But this one woman was very special, a lovely young woman. She was like a daughter to him. But she wouldn't give me the time of day, though I begged and pleaded."*

"Do you remember her name?" Mr. Abelman had asked.

"Certainly," Yuri Fedorov had said. *"How could I forget? Her name was Jelena Orlova."*

When Jupiter read this, it didn't mean anything in particular to him, but when he showed it to Mallory, her face lit up.

"Jelena Orlova?" she said. "That could have been the name on the card that went missing from the card catalogue! In fact, I'm almost sure it was. Remember what Bob said about it? He thought the name might be Helene. The two names are pretty close. Oreo and Orlova aren't close in the same way, but at least Bob was somewhere in the ballpark.

186

And now that I'm seeing the name myself, I'm almost 100% certain that was what it was. The card said, 'A gift from Jelena Orlova.'"

Jupiter remembered that Mallory had suggested that maybe the woman had written a dissertation.

"It doesn't say in the interview that she was a graduate student, or a Ph.D. candidate, or anything like that," Mallory said as she surfed the Net to see if she could find out anything about Jelena Orlova or her friendship with Vadim. She couldn't – until she checked out the death records for Los Angeles County and found that a woman named Jelena Orlova had died at the age of only fifty, of pneumonia. Her death was recorded as having happened seven years before.

Although they carefully read the interview transcripts to the end, they could find nothing else in them of apparent interest, and Jupiter suggested that Mallory call Mrs. Vasiliev and see if it would be all right if the two of them dropped by to ask her some questions. Mallory reached her at home, and when she seemed receptive to the idea, Mallory and Jupiter got on their bikes and bicycled to Mallory's apartment in the Wessex House. There, they left their bikes and walked around the corner.

When they knocked on Mrs. Vasiliev's door, it soon opened. Mrs. Vasiliev was wearing a flowered house dress and comfortable shoes.

"Come in, come in," she said. "It is so good to see you."

The apartment looked the same as it had the first time they'd visited, though the shades had not been pulled and the living room was flooded with light. When she saw Jupiter looking, she said, "Yes, I have let in the sun. So much more cheerful, don't you think? Will you have tea?"

Jupiter wanted to say no, but he knew that would be rude, so he told Mrs. Vasiliev he had been looking forward to it.

"Good," she said, bringing him a glass cup in a silver holder. "You remember how with the sugar cubes?" she said, gesturing to the silver dish on the coffee table. Jupiter hadn't quite gotten the hang of it the first time, but he stalwartly tried again.

"I see you are having trouble," she said mildly. "The young lady is doing better. Now, tell me. How do things go with your work? Have you beaten back the scourge of Colton Clark?"

"Not quite yet, Mrs. Vasiliev," Jupiter said, putting his tea down on the table. "But we're working on it."

"So you did not come to me to report?" she asked.

"Actually," Mallory said, "we have some questions for you. We wondered if you might have known a Russian émigré named Jelena Orlova."

"Jelena?" Mrs. Vasiliev said. "Yes, of course I knew her. She came over some years after Sasha and I did, when we were better established. Vadim Fedorov took a very great interest in her. She was younger than I was, by a good deal, and very pretty. Blondish-brown hair cut short and bright eyes. Good cheekbones."

Jupiter looked at her questioningly.

"She was a funny thing," Mrs. Vasiliev said. "Always trying to be positive, like an American. We Russians are prone to melancholia and tend to brood, but not Jelena. I could remember most everything that happened in Russia while I was there. Jelena not so much."

Mrs. Vasiliev seemed different today than she had when they'd first met her − more talkative and forthcoming. Of course there had been seven people in her apartment then, and today there were only two. Besides, the first visit had been an opportunity for the four of them to meet and talk to Ivan and Cassandra, and this visit was clearly about talking just to her.

"What do you remember?" Mallory asked her.

"So many things," Mrs. Vasiliev said. "But I would really prefer not to talk about them. Russia was so bad for so many for so long that any Russian who could move to America in those days was always happy he did. Scarcity, terror, and mass murder were Communism's main contributions to human history. I'm quoting a woman whose essay I read once, but I think she was just exactly right."

Mrs. Vasiliev poured herself more tea and sat down in an armchair facing the couch. "Under the czars, just a small group had power and money. But it was the exact same thing with Communism. Everyone was supposed to be equal, everyone was a comrade, but no. The leaders had everything and the people had nothing, even while the leaders' puppets were busy talking about 'justice' and 'equality.' It was a terrible system."

"But didn't people just live their lives and not pay so much attention to politics?" Mallory asked.

"Politics was everything and everything was politics," Mrs. Vasiliev said. "You could not read a book or see a movie, you could not go to a museum; you could not go to the laundromat! It was everywhere. If you did not think as you were told to think, you were punished."

"But surely some people spoke up," Jupiter said. "Surely people wanted to hear the truth."

"The truth was whatever the Party said it was, and the truth was constantly changing," Mrs. Vasiliev said. "Any disagreement was viciously repressed. If you had an idea that was against the government, you kept your mouth shut or went to prison or to the gulag. You were an enemy of the State and had committed a crime against the People."

Jupiter hadn't expected any of this. He'd been in search of specific information about Jelena Orlova and her friendship with Vadim Fedorov. But as he listened to Mrs. Vasiliev, he couldn't help but think about what she was saying, and how it might connect to Vadim Fedorov's lost novel. If the novel existed and could be found, it might be a truly amazing account of a man and woman – the writer's parents – who had escaped from the Soviet Union, then come to America, where their son − the writer − grew up to be accused of being a Soviet sympathizer.

Or something along those lines, Jupiter thought.

"But this isn't what you came to talk to me about today, is it?" said Mrs. Vasiliev.

"Not exactly," Jupiter said. "No."

"But then, if you hadn't been talking with Milan Szabó about what is happening in California because of this terrible Douglas Clark and others like him, I would never have met you in the first place. So it comes full circle," Mrs. Vasiliev said.

"You know about Douglas Clark?" Mallory asked.

"Of course, I do," Mrs. Vasiliev said. "If for no other reason than because this spawn of Satan who is trying to ruin Ivan's life is his son. I do not know how you would raise a child to grow up to act like this Colton Clark, but he did."

"Does this Jelena Orlova have any living relatives?" Mallory asked. "We discovered on the Internet that she died seven years ago."

"Yes," said Mrs. Vasiliev. "But she had not married and had no children." Mrs. Vasiliev shook her head sadly. "She was all alone in the world, really, except for Vadim, who was like a father to her and whose death hit her very hard."

She stared into the past, remembering. "And she was friends with another Russian émigré. When they were all alive, the three of them spent a good deal of time together, at Vadim's house or Ivan's. Yes, his name was Ivan, also, and as a matter of fact, I think that Yuri named his son after him. Though it is a very *very* common Russian name.

"Sometimes, after my Sasha died, I would spend time with him as well. But they are all gone now. It has been two years since Ivan died." She shook her head, as if wondering how such a thing was possible. "He died quite suddenly. Heart attack, I think. I did not know him all that well, but I did go to his house once. He bought it in the 1980s, in what was then not a very expensive part of the city — more on the outskirts, really. He was a surveyor and he did not make a lot of money."

She smiled, thinking about him. "He had some unusual hobbies," she said. "He loved to do needlepoint. He told me his mother had taught him, back in Russia, and when he sat pushing the needle through the fabric it brought him back to the days when he was a boy with his whole family around. He was also fascinated by the movies. His great-uncle had come to California from Russia after the revolution – at about the same time that Fyodor and Marinka came. This great-uncle was still alive when Ivan first came over, and he gave Ivan many things he had collected and kept from his work in the movies.

"In fact, this may have been how Vadim and Ivan met, because Ivan's great-uncle had worked on some of the same films that Vadim's father had acted in."

"What was Ivan's last name?" asked Jupiter.

"Ivanovich," said Mrs. Vasiliev, smiling. "His name was Ivan, son of Ivan."

"Mallory?" Jupiter said suddenly. "Would you look Ivan Ivanovich up?"

Mallory nodded. "Mrs. Vasiliev, I hope it's not rude," she said, "but would it be O.K. if I opened my laptop and did a little research?"

"Why, of course," Mrs. Vasiliev said. She smiled. "You young people and your computers!"

"I know what you mean, Mrs. Vasiliev," Jupiter said. "But they can be very useful, especially when you're trying to find things out quickly."

"Please, go ahead," the old woman said. "Do not mind me."

Jupiter moved to be closer to Mallory and watched as she typed in the name Ivan Ivanovich. As opposed to what had happened with Jelena Orlova, this time Mallory found fifteen hits in California, and three in the L.A. area. Since The Three Investigators subscribed to a service that, for a small monthly fee, gave a cursory search report on people's names, Mallory ordered one now, and when she got it, she and Jupiter saw a number of old addresses for various Ivan Ivanoviches. As he stared at one particular address, Jupiter got the feeling he'd seen it before. And not that long ago.

"Mallory?" he said again. "Do you have the address of Tracey Clark's house?"

"It's right here," Mallory said, taking out the address she'd been given. The addresses matched – but just to be certain, Mallory typed in the address of Tracey Clark's house again, on Zillow. Zillow didn't have any information about the name of the person from whom Tracey Clark had bought it, but by checking in the Los Angeles land records, Mallory found that the house that Tracey Clark had bought two years ago had, indeed, originally belonged to someone named Ivan Ivanovich.

As Jupiter stared at the name of the prior owner of Tracey Clark's house, he told himself to stay calm – not to leap to conclusions. But he found that difficult. He'd been involved with enough cases by this time in his life that he'd developed a second sense when things were accelerating toward the solution to a mystery.

There were coincidences that were really coincidences, and coincidences that weren't, and Jupiter knew that this one was the latter. The odds of Tracey Clark buying a house from the estate of a man who Vadim Fedorov had been friends with, and it having nothing to do with the case at hand were so slim as to be basically nonexistent.

It seemed that Mallory thought so, too, because she said, "I'd better call Cassandra. It looks as if I'm going to that writers' group meeting tonight."

10

Per Jorgensen Comes Through

Just at that moment – but on the other side of the city – Per Jorgensen was driving down the highway at the wheel of his vintage Jeep, a wonderfully boxy and mud-spattered vehicle of a rustic forest green. Ever since Jupiter had come up with the idea of asking the actor to help The Three Investigators interview Ivan and Colton's old classmates, Bob had felt a little concerned about whether they could keep Per busy and entertained, but he saw now he shouldn't have worried. Pete was doing an excellent job all on his own!

While Bob sat in the back, where Per kept a collection of dog-related paraphernalia – a metal water bowl with a black rubber rim, two leashes, a fleece blanket, and some bright yellow toys shaped like small footballs – Pete was in the front, talking non-stop.

Although the Jeep was a little rattly, Bob could hear that Pete was telling Per Jorgensen all about Vadim Fedorov and the lost novel The Three Investigators were looking for, and since Bob knew all about all of that already, as he stared at the dog stuff, he wondered what Brigitte – Per's German Shepherd – was up to today.

She was probably back at Per's house by the ocean; Bob supposed that Per very rarely, if ever, brought her with him when he came to the city. She was a great dog, Bob thought, and it had been funny when, the summer before, she'd helped The Three Investigators take down the German con man Günther Böhm.

Ahead of him, Bob saw the sign for Roosevelt High, and soon Per was turning into the parking lot.

"Here we are," Per said as the engine coughed itself silent. "And there they are."

He pointed to a small group of people talking together outside the high school's entrance. Some sat on a curved metal bench and the others stood around them. Bob thought it must be a sort of mini-reunion; they probably hadn't seen one another in a while. Now the ones who'd been sitting rose as if by command, and they all looked in the Jeep's direction, shading their eyes. As Per Jorgensen stepped down from the driver's seat, they became very still.

One of the women turned to another one and began whispering. One of the men crossed his arms on his chest. Bob remembered how *he'd* felt when he first met Per – tongue-tied, slightly dazed, and eager to be approved of. He supposed the people looking toward Per Jorgensen now felt the same. Jupiter had been right. Having Per ask the questions would really work to their advantage.

"Are we ready?" Per said, putting his arms around Pete's and Bob's shoulders for a moment. "I'm prepared to charm the truth out of these people." He smiled and started walking toward the crowd.

Per Jorgensen really was handsome, Bob thought as he tried to keep up with the man's stride. He had high cheekbones, a square chin, and dark hair streaked with blond from the sun, together with the regal glare of a hawk or eagle. But there was also something gentle in his gaze. Though he was probably in his early fifties, he looked much younger. You'd want him beside you in battle, but you'd also want him as your friend, Bob thought.

By the time Bob got to the metal bench, Per Jorgensen was already shaking hands and making small talk with Ivan's ex-classmates. There were seven of them, three men and four women, all in their early twenties – probably all twenty-three, the same age as Ivan. The men were dressed in tee shirts and jeans; several of the women wore summer dresses. As Per moved among them, they looked flustered, excited, almost dizzy.

After he had introduced himself to everyone, Per stepped back from the group. "Thank you all for coming," he said, in his wonderfully accented English. "These are my friends Bob Andrews and Pete Crenshaw. We'd like to ask each of you, one at a time, to answer some questions about your high school graduation party, O.K.?"

"That was at my house!" one of the women said, waving her hand. "I'm Helene Bobinski." Her hair was pulled back in a ponytail and she was wearing a short white skirt.

"Hello, Helene," Per said graciously. "Are you a tennis player?"

Per had melted into his role – a man who wanted nothing more in the world at the moment than to be probing the fascinating memories of seven people who had graduated high school five years earlier. Being one of the world's worst actors, Bob was envious but also quite amazed.

Helene almost swooned. "I play a little, yes," she said. "How did you know?"

Aside from her, Bob and the others had managed to locate Frank Tancredi and Billy

Osterman, who Ivan had mentioned, and also ex-classmates named Sheri Sanchez, Kashvi Kumar, Miguel Lopez, and Lisa Chen.

"Is there a place where we can sit down?" Per asked. "Some place a little more private than this lawn?" The idea of talking privately – or semi-privately – to Per Jorgensen was very appealing to almost all of them, Bob saw.

"Sure," one of the men said, pointing. Bob turned to see a metal canopy just off the parking lot, with two picnic tables under it.

"That's perfect," Per said, smiling. "Who'd like to go first?"

"Me!" one of the women said, almost tripping over herself in her haste to volunteer.

"And you are?" Per asked.

"Sheri," the woman said. "Sheri Sanchez." She had long black hair and a pert freckled nose. From her glee, she looked like she might have been the president of the southern California chapter of the Per Jorgensen Fan Club, Bob thought.

The four of them walked to one of the picnic tables under the metal canopy, Sheri Sanchez positioning herself as close to Per Jorgensen as possible. After they'd settled themselves, Bob took out his tape recorder and asked Sheri if it was O.K. to tape her. She nodded happily, as though it would be an honor. Bob also got out his notebook to take any additional notes. He pressed PLAY.

"Interview with Sheri Sanchez," he said. "Roosevelt High School. Conducted by Per Jorgensen, Bob Andrews, and Pete Crenshaw."

"Miss Sanchez," Per said, smiling. "I'd be grateful if you'd tell us what you remember about the party."

"Sure!" she said. "Hope I can help! I got there late, and – " To Bob's frustration, Sheri Sanchez's story didn't turn out to be that helpful. Though Per kept flattering her and asking questions, all she could remember was the band playing late into the evening and Colton Clark wearing a big sombrero.

"Was Ivan Fedorov playing with him?" Per asked. "Think carefully."

Sheri scrunched up her nose as though that helped her think. She shook her head. "I can't recall," she said.

"Thank you very much," Per said.

Bob clicked off the recorder.

"That's it?" she said, clearly disappointed she wouldn't get to spend more time staring into Per Jorgensen's eyes.

"I'm afraid so," Per Jorgensen said. "We

have six other people to talk to."

"Can I have your autograph?" she said impulsively, pulling a pad of paper from her purse.

"Of course," Per said. He smiled and complied.

The next person was Helene Bobinski herself. Bob asked for her permission and started taping again.

"Before we begin," she said, blushing, "I just have to say, Mr. Jorgensen, I really loved that movie, I can't remember the name of it, but it took place during the Second World War, and there were a lot of Nazis and you were against them, and you were so great!"

"*Tempest Island!*" said Pete.

"Why thank you," Per said. "I'm always glad to hear when someone enjoyed one of my movies."

"Enjoyed it?" Helene said. "I *loved* it!" She took a deep breath. "Well," she said. She talked about the party at great length – about how she'd tried to invite everyone in the class, but not everyone could come, of course, and how she'd been so busy as the host that she really couldn't remember in great detail when people had arrived and when they'd left. There was so much food! And people were jumping in the pool fully clothed! Ivan had been there, of course; she remembered talking to him. But whether he'd gone home early – well, she just couldn't say.

"We're not really getting anywhere, are we?" Pete said after she had left.

"I wouldn't worry," Per said. "We've just gotten started."

Billy Osterman was more helpful. He, too, had something to say about one of Per's movies – in his case, it was *The Seventh Messenger.* "That medieval epic thing you starred in. You were cool, dude. Great swordplay." – but when asked, he said, "It was a good party. Everyone was chill, you know what I mean? When it finally got dark, about quarter to ten, the band started jamming – Colton Clark and some of his friends. They sounded pretty good."

"Do you remember who his friends were?" Per asked.

"Yeah," Osterman said. "I was pretty stoned and I lay down in a lounge chair and watched them for a long time. Kenny Blatz was on drums and I think Johnny Del Rio was on keyboards. Or was it bass?"

"Was Ivan Fedorov playing with them?" Per asked.

"Fedorov?" Osterman said. "Nah. He

wasn't there."

"Are you positive?" Bob asked.

"Yeah," Osterman said. "I was stoned, but I'm totally certain. I really love music."

Well, Bob thought. That was something.

Frank Tancredi clearly wasn't sure who Per Jorgensen was, but he was happy to answer questions. He remembered seeing Ivan talking to Colton Clark at the party, but he couldn't remember if it was before dark or after dark. It had been a long time, he said. Five years! Who could believe five years had passed since they'd graduated from high school? And now he'd graduated from college with a degree in civil engineering and had gotten a job working for the city of Santa Monica. But Ivan was a great guy. He'd really liked Ivan, Tancredi said. Colton Clark, not so much. He was a playground bully – the kind who pushed you off the jungle gym in second grade.

Kashvi Kumar remembered Ivan well from the party. They'd sat down together early on when the grills were in full swing and people were eating burgers and cole slaw and pickles. He seemed so Russian to her, a bit melancholy – but then they were all a bit melancholy about the end of high school. They were glad, of course. High school had been a drag. But it had also been safe, you know? And the future was scary.

"Do you remember when the music started?" Per asked.

"Yes," Kashvi said. "After it got dark. I didn't like it much. Too jarring. They were just fooling around, I think. They didn't sound like they'd practiced."

"Was Ivan playing with Colton Clark?" Per asked.

"Ivan?" she said. "I don't think so, but I couldn't say for sure. But it wouldn't have been his thing. He's a very polished musician."

Bob was getting a little discouraged. Five years wasn't really that long, and yet memories blurred, people forgot, newer memories over-wrote the older ones. There were still two more people to talk to. They needed more corroborating witnesses – hopefully unstoned ones!

Lisa Chen said that her boyfriend at the time had been good friends with Johnny Del Rio, and she remembered watching when they started jamming after it got dark. There were spotlights in the trees, and she'd seen them very clearly. Colton Clark had been the lead, making stupid small talk into the mic from time to time, bowing a lot. The music had been O.K., nothing too special. Some people had been dancing.

"Do you remember who else was in the band aside from Del Rio and Clark?" Per asked.

"I can't remember their names," Lisa Chen said. "One of them was on the track team."

"How about Ivan Fedorov?" Pete asked. "Did you know him?

"Did I know him?" Lisa said. "Sure. Everyone knew Ivan."

"Was he playing with the band?" Bob asked.

"No," Lisa said. "Definitely not. Definitely not."

Bingo, Bob thought. But the best was yet to come.

Miguel Lopez had spiky black hair and an easy grin. He looked like an athlete − maybe a runner, Bob thought. He seemed particularly comfortable with Per.

"I left the party," Miguel said, "and went out to my car. It was still early, and I wanted to get my yearbook so that people could sign it before things got out of hand."

"Do you remember the time?" Per asked.

"Eight o'clock?" Miguel said. "People

had pretty much finished eating and the sun was going down. I ran into Ivan out on the street. He was parked right behind me. He said he had to leave early."

"And the music hadn't started yet?" Per Jorgensen said.

"The music?" Miguel said. "No. That didn't start until after it got real dark. Like ten o'clock."

"And you're sure it was Ivan," Per said.

"Absolutely," Miguel said. "I told him I was sorry he had to leave so early. He was staring out at the sunset and he mentioned how beautiful the sky looked. I agreed. Ivan's a great songwriter and I made a cheesy suggestion. I said if he liked the sunset so much, maybe he should write a song about the sunset of our high school years."

He looked a little embarrassed. "Ivan thought that was funny. He laughed and said maybe he would. I watched him as he got in his car and drove away. I don't think I've seen him since. I wonder if he ever wrote that song." He paused and looked at Per. "I remember it as if it was yesterday."

Bob knew exactly what Miguel meant. Sometimes something perfectly ordinary got stuck in your memory because the details surrounding it were so vivid. The sunset, the year-book, the cars, the conversation – all of it had settled in Miguel's mind, and his story had the ring of absolute truth. The connection Miguel had made between the end of the day and the end of high school had helped a lot. Here was the testimony they needed that Ivan had left the party early and couldn't have played with Colton Clark. It was a lie that Clark had made up to enable his blackmail.

"Thank you very much," Per Jorgensen said, standing and shaking Miguel's hand. "You've been extremely helpful. If it comes to it, would you testify to what you just told us under oath?"

Miguel looked startled, "Sure," he said. "I guess so."

From the minute Miguel Lopez walked away, Per shed the persona he'd been wearing during the interview. Bob was amazed at the transformation. Before, he'd been overly eager, almost wide-eyed in his enthusiasm. Now he started being himself again, far more natural, laid-back, and relaxed. He was a very good actor, Bob thought.

"I think that should help Ivan," he said, leading the way back to his Jeep.

"You did it, Mr. Jorgensen," Pete said.

"We couldn't have done it without you."

"Oh, I think you could have," Per said, opening the car door. "But it was my pleasure. And how am I going to get you to stop calling me Mr. Jorgensen?"

Pete clambered into the front passenger seat of the Jeep, and Bob was just about to climb back into the back when Sheri Sanchez rushed up to him and pulled his arm.

"Can I talk to you for a minute?" she said. "Alone? It's important."

"Sure," Bob said as he let himself be dragged away from the Jeep. He glanced over his shoulder to see Pete and Per looking at him questioningly. When they were about fifty feet away, Sheri started talking, looking at Bob intently.

"I was so embarrassed," she said. "When he" – she nodded her head in Per's direction – "when he asked me at the end if I had any other information I wanted to share about Colton Clark, I just couldn't say anything. I mean, clearly he didn't like Colton, and I – " She paused and took a deep breath.

"Listen," she said. "When we were in high school I dated Colton for a while. He was really a creep. He pretended to be friendly with Ivan in school but made fun of him behind his back."

"When was this?" Bob asked.

"All during senior year," Sheri Sanchez said. "I think Colton was jealous because Ivan's music was way better than his. He criticized the way Ivan looked and made fun of his family. He called them a bunch of Russkies."

"Russkies?" Bob said.

"Russkies," she said. "Like that was the worst thing to be on earth. He had a cousin who lived down the street from a Russian guy named Ivan Ivanovich, and when Colton was twelve or thirteen, he and his cousin were walking down the street and this Ivanovich was out mowing his lawn. The cousin liked Ivan and started talking to him about a detective movie he'd just seen, and Ivan Ivanovich mentioned that he'd been friends with a great mystery writer – the famous Edison Ford. Even Colton had heard of Edison Ford, and he told me he might have been impressed if it wasn't for the fact that his cousin had told him that Ivan Ivanovich did needlepoint!

"Colton said he knew that Edison Ford had to have been hard-nosed and macho and would never have been friends with a sissy who did needlepoint. Therefore, Ivan Ivanovich had to be lying about knowing Edison Ford, and from there Colton concluded that all Russkies were liars — and maybe thieves. I can't believe I kept dating him even after that. That's all I can tell you, but please don't tell Mr. Jorgensen."

Bob promised he wouldn't.

As Bob settled in the back seat, Pete turned around. "What was that about?" he asked.

"Never mind," Bob said, "I'll tell you later." In a way, he wished he could tell them now, but since he'd promised Sheri Sanchez not to tell Per, it would have to wait.

"Well," Pete said. "At least it looks like we finally got what we need to help Ivan."

"But we still haven't found the missing novel," Bob said. "I hope that Mallory and Jupiter have come up with some clues that will help us find it."

"Yeah," Pete said. "How come there aren't more copies of it? You'd think there'd be hundreds."

Per Jorgensen looked over at him, amused. "Vadim Fedorov started writing before there were copy machines," he said. "Back in the 1930s and 1940s, screenwriters like Vadim Fedorov always worked on a typewriter and made three copies of their work. They interwove two sheets of carbon paper between the top sheet and two other sheets of paper – making three copies at once."

"But Vadim didn't keep writing screenplays!" said Pete. "He was blacklisted in the 1950s and switched over to writing detective novels."

"Even so," said Per. "If it was still the 1950s when he switched to novels, he would have had to keep using a typewriter to write on, and he probably also just kept up his old screenwriting habit of making three copies."

"But wouldn't the lost novel have been typed on a computer?" Bob asked.

"Maybe," said Per, "but I doubt it. You said Vadim was born in 1920, and even though computers pushed typewriters out in the 1990s, by that time he would have been in his 70s. He probably never used a computer but kept typing his books right up until he died."

"But what about copy machines?" Pete asked.

"Well, there you have me," said Per. "Copy machines were around by the 1970s, so there's really no reason why he wouldn't have been able to make as many copies as he liked. In fact, he must have made copies to send to his agent and publisher. But if this novel wasn't finished yet, that might not have come into it for him."

"It's hard to imagine a world without copy machines," Pete said.

"That may be so," Per said, "but it did exist."

"Three copies, at least," Bob said. "And we don't know where any of them are."

"Yet," Pete said with a grin.

Just then, Bob's cellphone rang, and when he saw it was Mallory calling, he flipped it open and put it on speakerphone.

"Mallory," he said. "We've got really good news. Per was totally great in talking to Ivan's old classmates, and Ivan should have no trouble getting Colton Clark to drop the lawsuit. Or the threat of one. Two of the people we interviewed remembered the party very clearly and in great detail. Both of them said that as the party went on and it got dark, Colton and some of his friends were jamming under the lights by the pool."

"And Ivan wasn't with them!" Pete called over his shoulder. "So whatever music Colton was playing, Ivan never even heard it, much less stole it!"

"That *is* great news!" Mallory said.

As they rattled down the highway, Bob went on. "Both the people we talked to are willing to swear – in an affidavit if it comes to that – that Ivan wasn't in the group with Colton. One of them actually even remembered Ivan leaving the party early – long before the music started." He told Mallory about the way the yearbook, the sunset, the cars, and the talk with Ivan had all fixed the memory in his mind.

"I know just what the guy means," Mallory said. "That's really great. Listen, I'm calling to tell you that Jupiter and I are at my place – at the Wessex House – because we've decided I should go to Tracey Clark's book party this afternoon after all, and Cassandra's going to pick me up here. Just call me when you get to the Salvage Yard, and Jupiter will bike back to meet you there."

Per had been listening and now he said to Pete and Bob, "Why don't I just drop you off at Mallory's place instead of the Salvage Yard? That way the four of you can talk in person."

"That would be great," Bob said.

To Mallory, he added, "Did you hear that?" and she said "Yes. That would be brilliant."

"How did things go with the transcripts? And at Mrs. Vasiliev's?" Bob asked.

"Really well," Mallory said. "We found

out that Tracey Clark's house originally belonged to a friend of Vadim Fedorov's – a Russian émigré called Ivan Ivanovich – and that seemed so suspicious I knew I had to go to this writers' group meeting."

"Tracey Clark bought the house of a Russian émigré named Ivan Ivanovich?" Bob asked excitedly. He wished more than ever that he could tell the story Sheri Sanchez had told him, but it wouldn't be long before they got to the Wessex House now. Maybe fifteen or twenty more minutes.

"I actually know something about that," he said. "So don't leave for the writers' group meeting before Pete and I get there!"

"I won't," Mallory said. "But what's going on? What do you know?"

"I can't really say at the moment – " Bob started, just as his cellphone suddenly cut off. He held it up and saw it was out of juice, but as he retrieved a power adaptor from his pocket and plugged it into the cigarette lighter in the console of Per Jorgensen's Jeep, he wasn't unduly concerned. He and Pete would be arriving at the Wessex House soon, and when they got there, he could tell Mallory what Sheri Sanchez had told him privately in the parking lot of Roosevelt High.

11

Mallory Dials Headquarters

In the meanwhile, on the porch of the Wessex House where Mallory and Jupiter were sitting side by side, Mallory was talking to a dead phone.

"Hello?" Mallory said. "Bob, are you there?" She turned to Jupiter. "We've been cut off. His battery must have died. Oh, well, they'll be here soon."

All of them, she realized. Including Per Jorgensen – who she liked a lot, but who also made her a little tongue-tied and who she hadn't been expecting to see today.

After getting back from Mrs. Vasiliev's, Mallory had called Cassandra and told her what she and Jupiter had discovered.

"It's a strange coincidence," Mallory had explained – that Tracey Clark had bought Ivan Ivanovich's house – "so strange that it can't be a coincidence really. I think I need to go to your writing group so I can snoop around and see what I can find out."

Cassandra had offered to pick Mallory up, and Mallory had gratefully accepted. After that, she and Jupiter had had some lunch and then come out to the porch to talk. Before Mallory had called Bob, they'd been discussing what they'd learned about Jelena Orlova.

By now, Mallory was totally certain that Jelena Orlova had been the name on the card that Tracey Clark had ripped out of the card catalogue. Her hypothesis that maybe Orlova had written a paper or a dissertation or something about Fyodor Fedorov had dissolved when she discovered that Orlova was never a graduate student, or a Ph.D. candidate, or anything like that. Mallory and Jupiter had agreed almost at once that what Jelena Orlova had donated to the American Film History Library must have been a copy of Vadim Fedorov's lost novel.

In fact, they were now both as certain of this as you *could* be of an as-yet-untested hypothesis, and after Mallory checked to make sure that her own cellphone was fully charged, she picked up the conversation where she and Jupiter had left off.

"So you think Vadim Fedorov gave a copy of his novel to his friend Jelena, and that when she donated it to the library, she wasn't aware that the original had been lost?" Mallory said.

"I think that must be it," Jupiter said. "This morning, it occurred to me that maybe the novel wasn't found in Vadim's house or among his papers because he'd sent the only copy he still had off to the Copyright Office in Washington D.C.

"That would have been before everything was digitized, and from what I can tell, it's nearly impossible to track down something sent to the Copyright Office in those days. Besides, we don't know the title! Anyway, I had no luck."

"It's too bad the film library is closed today," Mallory said. "If it were open, we could just call Mr. Abelman and ask him to go into the stacks and see if he can find an archive box with Foderov, V. on it!"

"Yes," said Jupiter, pinching his lower lip. "You know, I keep thinking about the scene in *Dawn Over Petrograd* in which Fyodor Fedorov lifted down the book with the hammer and sickle. I mean, it was a *book*."

Mallory looked at Jupiter with interest. "Fyodor was Vadim's father, after all, and Vadim undoubtedly saw *Dawn Over Petrograd* a number of times when he was growing up. Not only that, but his father probably told him, with pleasure, about the clues he had woven into the film."

What Jupiter was implying dawned on Mallory.

"You mean – ," she said.

"Yes," said Jupiter. "Exactly." He steepled his fingers and nodded. "What if Vadim decided that the title of the book his father had in his hand when he played the Bolshevik character would be a great title for the novel he was writing – a novel about what had happened to his parents as a result of the Russian Revolution? What if the title of Vadim Fedorov's lost novel is *The Intemperate Imperium?*"

Mallory looked at Jupiter in admiration. "Of course!" she said. "You're incredible, Jupiter! Really!"

Although Mallory had been about to call Jupiter a genius, at the final instant she used the word "incredible" instead. Bob had mentioned to her several times how much Jupiter hated having Pete "exaggerate," as Jupiter put it. Jupiter smiled modestly at the compliment – just as a boxy vintage Jeep pulled around the corner and headed toward the Wessex House.

Luckily, Mallory didn't need to figure out how to act around Per today, because he said he had to get going, and all she and Jupiter had time to say was hello and goodbye.

They all thanked Per again for his help, and as he took off down the street while the four of them waved, he thrust his hand out the driver's side window and followed with a toot on the Jeep's horn.

The four of them went inside. As they passed Mallory's bedroom, Pete peeked through the door. "You still have the immigrant's chest!" he said.

"Are you kidding?" Mallory said. "I'll always have that chest. I adore it." It had been almost exactly a year since Pete, Bob, and Jupiter had presented her with a chest that Leif and Magnus, the Salvage Yard's resident carpenters, had made and a local artist had painted – using the pattern of a chest she'd seen and liked in a bookstore where she'd met The Three Investigators by accident.

She'd known soon after she'd met them how special Pete, Bob and Jupiter were, but the gift of that chest had really thrilled her, and she was happy to look at it every night before she went to sleep.

At the moment, however, as they settled into the living room, she wanted to know what Bob had meant on the phone when he'd said he couldn't talk just then.

"You told me you knew something about

Tracey Clark and Ivan Ivanovich," she said.

Bob nodded. "One of the girls we talked to was Colton Clark's girlfriend for a while."

"What?" said Pete. "I didn't hear that!"

"Well, *we* didn't talk to her," Bob went on, "because she was embarrassed to say that in front of Per Jorgensen. But you saw the way she pulled me aside just before we left. She told me she'd dated Colton. No happy memories, it seems. She said that Colton pretended to be friendly with Ivan in school but dissed him behind his back, mocking the way he looked and making fun of his family. She thought Colton was jealous because Ivan was a way better musician than he was."

Mallory already had many reasons to dislike Colton Clark, but these new details burned her particularly. She hated meanness.

"Anyway," Bob said, "she told me a story about Colton and a cousin of his and Tracey's. The cousin was friends with an older Russian guy named Ivan Ivanovich who knew Vadim Federov. The cousin liked to talk with him about movies. I guess Ivanovich loved movies.

"Yes," Mallory said. "That's what Mrs. Vasiliev told us."

"When his cousin mentioned to Colton

that Ivanovich knew Edison Ford, Colton was really impressed. Until he heard that Ivan did needlepoint, and then his head exploded. Can you believe that?" Bob said.

"Only too easily," Mallory said.

"So when you called with the news about Ivan Ivanovich's house, I saw right away that the cousin was probably the one who told Tracey about Ivan Ivanovich dying and the house being on the market," Bob said. "Since Tracey said that Colton and a cousin were going to be at this writing group, I'm thinking it might be the same cousin. If so, you might get a lot of information out of him."

"That's a great idea, Bob," Mallory said. She glanced at her watch. "Cassandra should be here soon, but I just realized that you don't have a way to get back to the Salvage Yard. Jupiter has his bike, but the two of you don't. One of you could take my bike, I guess, and my mother has a bike. Why don't you take them both? I'd ask Cassandra to drive you, but we're heading in the opposite direction, and I want to get to Tracey's house on time."

"That should work fine," said Pete. "Thanks!"

Shortly after the boys biked off, Cassandra arrived. Mallory told her about Per's interviews with Ivan's classmates, and Cassandra was overjoyed.

By the time they got to Tracey Clark's, it was almost four o'clock. The house was on a quiet street, far from the freeways, with narrow well-landscaped lots. Cassandra found a place to park right in front, and Mallory followed her around the house and through a wooden gate in a low and tasteful fence to the backyard, where most of the members of the writers' group had already assembled.

Mallory could see Colton Clark and someone roughly his age working near a grill on the other side of the pool. She watched as Colton piled the briquettes, squirted too much lighter fluid, and then stepped back and threw a match on the pyre, erupting in hyena-like laughter when a pillar of fire shot into the air.

What a jerk, she thought.

Under one of the trees to the side of the pool, a group of mostly women had settled into plastic outdoor chairs, holding laptops, tablets, and sheets of paper.

"Go on," Mallory said. "Join your friends. I'll come in a moment. I just want to check out the cousin."

She walked around the pool until she came to the grill. Colton looked at her suspiciously.

"You again," he said. "Did you just come with Cassandra Abelman?"

"Yes," Mallory said. "I'm still doing research for the paper I told you about, so I was talking to Cassandra. But your sister invited me because I was interested in the book she was writing."

Mallory decided to act a bit younger than she was – a bit wide-eyed and naïve.

"Hi," the cousin said. "Colton will never introduce me so I'll introduce myself. I'm Billy. Billy Davis." He offered his hand and Mallory shook it. He had a friendly open face and didn't seem like the type who'd hang around with Colton. "Would you like a soda?"

"Sure," Mallory said. "That would be nice."

"Where are you from?" he asked.

"I live in Rocky Beach," Mallory said.

"No," he said. "I meant what country."

Mallory laughed. "I grew up in Scotland but I moved back here with my mother about a year ago. What about you?"

"I'm a local," he said grinning. "I live right down the street, where I grew up. I'm still living with my parents until I make enough money to move out."

"He's a deadbeat," Colton said. "Runs in the family."

"*Your* family," Billy said. "You've never had a job in your life."

Colton grinned as though he was proud of the fact. Mallory did her best to ignore him. "This is a great place," she said, looking back at the house. "When did Tracey buy it?"

"About two years ago," Billy said. "A really nice old guy lived here. He was from Russia, originally, but he came to this country before I was born. He was really smart and took great care of the place."

"I called him Russkie Russkievich," Colton said.

"Shut up, Colton," Billy said. "You can be such a jerk." He shook his head in disgust. "His name was Ivan Ivanovitch," he explained

"Did you tell Tracey about the house when it went on the market?" Mallory asked.

"Guilty," Billy said. "When Ivan died, I told Tracey she should take a look at the place. I used to talk to him several times a week, I guess. We talked a lot about the movies, and he knew just about everything. He had a relative who'd worked in Hollywood for a long time, with costumes or props or sets or something. Not an actor.

226

"He invited me in once. He collected old movie memorabilia, clippings from the newspapers about movies and movie stars, photographs, old posters, stuff like that. He kept the yard real nice, but the inside was a bit of a mess. Boxes of papers, magazines. I guess he was a pack rat."

"Gee," Mallory said. "It sounds like there was a lot of clearing out to do."

"Some," Billy said, "but Tracey wound up buying most of the stuff with the house. Ivan's relatives back in Russia sold it all to her for $5000."

Colton suddenly glowered at him. "Why don't you shut your yap," he said, "and come over here and help me. And stop flirting. She's just a kid."

Billy rolled his eyes.

"It was nice meeting you," Mallory said, sincerely. "Thanks for the soda." She'd wound up liking Billy Davis. He'd been extremely helpful and she was more determined than ever to get inside the house and look around.

She wandered over and joined the writing group.

"Here we go again," one of few men said as she sat down, gesturing with his head toward Tracey who was handing out sheafs of paper stapled together. Mallory wondered what he meant and asked him.

"Oh," he said, seeming surprised at her question. "Just a little quirk of Tracey's. The rest of us send our work to one another electronically, but she's a stickler for old-school. Always paper copies and she always collects them at the end of the session, in case we've written down any comments or suggestions. Also, she says she doesn't want old drafts floating around. I guess I can see what she means."

Meanwhile Tracey had reached the small group Mallory was with.

"Mallory," she said in a bright warm voice. "You made it. Here's a copy of the chapter we'll be talking about."

"Thanks," Mallory said. She glanced down at the pages she'd been given as Tracey wandered away and let her eyes drift over the paragraphs. They were written in the third person, and the action all took place inside the mind of a middle-aged Russian woman – showing what she saw and heard and thought.

From the details, which were surprisingly acute, Mallory could see that the scene was set in a bookstore in Hollywood in the 1930s. She instantly liked the character, who was a bit melancholy but very smart, and the writing was excellent. Mallory was impressed but also suspicious, and she remembered the conversation she'd overheard at Cassandra's book party about how much Tracey's writing had improved. How could anyone go from bad to good so quickly, without anything in between?

Still, what really struck her was how fully Tracey seemed to have captured the mindset of someone completely different from herself – a Russian émigré who was fervently anti-Communist, while Tracey had grown up comfortably in southern California, happy to take whatever was handed to her, and with a father who seemed to find socialism a comfortable fit. Mallory would have thought that this sort of imaginative empathy would be beyond someone like Tracey Clark.

After a period of restless silence, broken only by the shuffling of pages as they read, the group's comments were uniformly supportive as they talked about how subtly Tracey was able to reveal her character's attitude toward the pro-Communist she'd met at the bookstore, how the details of her clothing and appearance communicated her mental state. No one had any criticisms, and the majority of comments were congratulations.

Tracey looked pleased, thanked everyone, and reminded them to give the pages back to her at the end of the meeting, with any written comments they might have.

Carefully, and without anyone seeing her, Mallory folded the pages and slipped them into her pants pocket. Then, as the group readied itself to move on to the work of another writer, Mallory walked over to Tracey and asked if she could use the bathroom.

"Of course," Tracey said. "It's on the first floor, in the front."

Mallory entered the house through a door that led into a back hall. Inside, the house was cool and quiet. Mallory listened carefully, making sure she was the only one there. She walked down the hall, past the kitchen and dining room, and into the living room.

She was surprised to see a number of framed movie posters on the walls, some of them quite old. When she looked closely, she saw that several of them starred Fyodor Fedorov. In a shadow box on the wall hung a black ceramic cross, depending from a ribbon, with gold double-headed eagles, very much like the medal Fyodor's character had worn in *Dawn Over Petrograd.*

It suddenly dawned on Mallory that Ivan Ivanovich's great-uncle had almost certainly been the crew member who had helped Fyodor express his true political leanings in the movie. Of course! she thought excitedly.

She was startled when the back door banged and she turned around to see Billy Davis.

"Oh, hi," he said. "I just came in to get some more ice. Were you looking at the posters? They're cool, aren't they? They belonged to Ivan, and Tracey bought them with the house."

"They're very cool," Mallory said. "They look like originals, not even reproductions."

"They are," Billy said. "Ivan got them from his relative."

"Are there other things in the house that belonged to Ivan?" Mallory asked.

"I'm sure there are, somewhere. I know there's a footstool that belonged to him. Tracey keeps it underneath her writing desk to prop her feet on."

When Billy looked a little embarrassed, Mallory said, "What?"

"It's just that the footstool's embroidered," he said. "Ivan did needlepoint. I know. Most people think – "

"I think it's great," Mallory said. "I really admire people who are good with their hands.

Could I see it?"

Billy smiled. "Sure," he said. "I don't see why not. Tracey wouldn't mind. Follow me." He led her down a hallway and into a room with a long wooden desk on which a closed laptop sat next to a printer. Billy got down on his hands and knees and from underneath the desk he pulled out a three-legged stool with a deep chocolate brown top.

Mallory gasped. Billy Davis looked at her approvingly.

"It's really something, isn't it?" he asked.

On the heavy brown fabric, Ivan Ivanovich had embroidered a hammer and sickle just like the hammer and sickle on the spine of the book Fyodor Fedorov had lifted down from the bookshelf in *Dawn Over Petrograd*. In addition, he'd embroidered an eagle – and not the double-headed imperial eagle of Russia but the iconic bald eagle of the United States! Best of all, below the hammer and sickle and the eagle, he'd embroidered words in both Cyrillic and English – and the English words read *The Intemperate Imperium*!

"Wow!" said Mallory, thinking quickly. It was as if Ivan Ivanovich had been trying to make a point – that both the Soviet Union and the United States of America could be seen as unrestrained empires.

"Did Ivan Ivanovich like this country?" she asked Billy.

"He loved it. Land of opportunity," he said in an attempt at a bad Russian accent. "But not so much the foreign wars."

Mallory was down on her knees, examining the stool more closely when there was the sound of footsteps behind her and she turned to see Tracey Clark staring at her, frowning.

"Might I ask what you're doing in my study?" she said. "I thought you came in to use the bathroom." She looked annoyed and – at least if Mallory was right – a little worried.

"I did," Mallory said. "I – "

"It's my fault, Tracey," Billy said gallantly. "I told her before about Ivan Ivanovich and she was interested in – "

Tracey stepped out of the way and ushered Mallory and Billy back into the hall. Trying to smile pleasantly, she said, "No harm done. Did you ever find the bathroom?"

"No," Mallory said.

"If you still need it," Tracey said, "it's right down here." She gestured to a closed door.

"Thank you," Mallory said. She went in, closed and locked the door behind her, and sat down on the toilet seat, suddenly breathless. Tracey Clark had not been happy to find her staring at that stool, Mallory thought. She was trying to hide something. She stared at the walls until her heart calmed down.

An idea was nagging at her, quite hard, but it remained elusive. In her mind it was like a shadow she kept chasing, and whenever she got close, it slipped away. Maybe the boys could help her, she thought, as she slipped her cellphone out of her pocket. She turned on the water in the sink to muffle the sound of her voice.

But before she could dial, she heard a loud, rude, inconsiderate blaring in the street, someone leaning on a car horn. She stood up and looked out the already-open window.

The bathroom was on the side of the house facing the street, and she watched as a car pulled up with a screech and another blaring of the horn and two young men got out. Their hair was slicked back and their eyes were hidden behind dark glasses. They wore jeans and sleeveless tee-shirts. They had broad shoulders and cartoon biceps. One of them wore a red bandana around his forehead.

Mallory wasn't sure, but he looked like Colton's friend from the book party – the one who had tried to steal a guitar from Ivan's van.

As she watched, Colton Clark came bounding from the back yard, presumably in response to the horn.

"Dudes!" he shouted as he high-fived one and then the other. There was a good deal of laughing. Mallory shut her phone and crouched in front of the window, straining to hear.

She heard the word "library," and then one of Colton's friends said, "So how much is this book worth?"

"A lot," Colton said. "I'll give twenty per cent of whatever Tracey gives me to each of you if we can get it."

"And sixty percent to you?" the other one said. Mallory was surprised he could do the math so quickly. "Hell, no. Get out of here. Thirty per cent to each of us or we split."

"O.K.," Colton said, raising his hands in an attempt to mollify them. "We'll talk about it."

"Why does she want to burn it?" the first one asked.

"Stop asking questions," Colton said. "Let's get moving."

The idea Mallory had been stalking, the elusive shadow, stepped forward into the light.

She watched Colton jump in the car, and the three of them took off with a screech of tires. Mallory flipped open her cellphone and frantically dialed Headquarters.

12

A Crucial Revelation

Jupiter was sitting with Pete and Bob when the phone rang. It was stuffy in Headquarters, and he'd only managed to get his friends to join him by saying that he had a hunch that Mallory would call, and it would be better if they could just put her on the landline's speakerphone.

When they'd first gotten back to the Salvage Yard, they'd wandered down to Jupiter's house to get something for Bob and Pete to eat – Pete was starving! – and had wound up putting together peanut butter and banana sandwiches. They'd finished eating now and had come inside.

Jupiter didn't know exactly why he couldn't relax. He understood that part of it was his lingering frustration at not being able to get his hands on what he fully believed was the manuscript of Vadim Fedorov's missing novel. But part of it, he suspected, was Mallory.

Though what she'd set out to do wasn't dangerous on the face of it, he didn't know what she might find in Tracey Clark's house or

237

how badly Tracey or Colton Clark wouldn't want her to find it. He vaguely remembered a proverb he'd heard about the den of a lion, but he couldn't remember the words.

He thought for a minute about the successes of the day. He'd been pleased to learn from Pete and Bob how easy it would be to gather the testimony that Ivan's lawyer would need to brush away Colton Clark and his bogus lawsuit. Jupiter had been feeling vaguely guilty from the start at how uninterested he was in the case – not in helping Ivan, of course, but in the means he needed to employ to do so.

Finding out peoples' names and addresses, talking to them – this involved none of the skills that he most enjoyed using, though it might have required both tact and cunning if the interview subjects had been at all devious or resistant. But apparently, with Per Jorgensen asking the questions, the interviews had been quite straightforward.

In fact, Bob had told him, every single one of the people he, Pete, and Per had talked to had been cheerful, forthcoming, and happy to help. If they'd had to pick sides, each of them would have gone with Ivan Fedorov, Bob said. It seemed Colton Clark had not been very good at making friends.

Still, Jupiter had to face up to the fact that he hadn't approached this case the way he should have, and he still felt a bit of lingering guilt about being more interested in the lost novel than in the threat to Ivan's happiness. Now he saw no need to feel guilty any more, which was a relief.

Nevertheless, he was still feeling a little on edge when the landline in Headquarters started ringing. He glanced at his watch. It was not yet 7:00, when the writing group was supposed to end. He punched speakerphone. "Three Investigators Headquarters," he said. "Jupiter Jones speaking."

"Jupiter?" Mallory's tense voice came over the speaker. "Thank goodness you're there."

Both Bob and Pete heard the worry in her voice and sat forward in their chairs.

"We're all here, Mallory," Jupiter said. "Is everything O.K.?"

"I'm O.K.," Mallory said. "But I can't say everything's O.K."

"What do you mean?" Jupiter asked.

"If I'm right in my deductions, Vadim Fedorov's manuscript is in danger."

"What's going on?" Pete asked, alarmed.

"I was in Tracey Clark's house when a

loud car with two over-muscled lowlifes pulled up on the street outside. I could see and hear everything," Mallory said. "Colton came out to meet them. He got in the car and they roared off. But before they did, I heard them talking — just enough for me to think they're planning to head over to the library to steal whatever may be in the archive box and maybe burn it."

"What?" Pete said. "They can't. The library's closed on Wednesday and even if it was open, it'd be closed by now."

"I don't have time to explain the whole thing," Mallory said, "but if I'm right, you better get in touch with Mr. Abelman as soon as possible and see if he can meet us at the library. I heard Colton tell his thug friends that they'd get a cut of the money Tracey was paying him to steal whatever it is they're stealing. I'll tell Cassandra my mother called and needs me to come home right away, but when we're in the car I'll tell her the truth. She can bring me to the Salvage Yard and hopefully drive us all over to the library."

"But they can't get in!" Pete said again. "The library's closed! It's locked! Besides, the manuscript's restricted."

"That may be so," Mallory said. "But remember that security guard we ran into? He got the job through Colton's father. And he works on Wednesdays. If he's meeting them to let them in, then we've really got to hurry. I've got more to tell you – a *lot* more – but the rest of it can wait. What matters is you calling Mr. Abelman."

"Good work, Mallory," Jupiter said. "Get here as fast as you can."

In his mind's eye he saw her hurrying outside and acting as though nothing was wrong as she got Cassandra to leave the writing group. He pinched his bottom lip. Why did Tracey Clark want to destroy the manuscript of what was almost certainly Vadim Fedorov's missing novel? An idea was beginning to form.

He stood up abruptly, sending the swivel chair he'd been sitting in rocketing backward against the wall. He was suddenly very anxious. Colton Clark and his thugs had the clear advantage. They were already on their way to the library, and Jupiter, Pete, and Bob would have to wait for Cassandra to give them a ride. Not only that, but first she'd have to drive Mallory all the way back to the Salvage Yard. He hoped that they wouldn't be too late!

"Bob," he said, "could you send a text to Mr. Abelman, asking him to call us here? We need to let him know what's happening."

Bob took out his cellphone and Jupiter watched as his thumbs flew over the buttons.

It took almost no time for Mr. Abelman to call. "Jupiter!" he said. "Is something the matter?"

"I'm afraid so, Mr. Abelman," Jupiter said. "I just heard on good authority that Colton Clark is on his way to the library. I think he intends to get his hands on a copy of Vadim Fedorov's lost novel – a copy donated to the library by his friend Jelena Orlova. Yuri Fedorov talked about her in one of the interviews you did with him, and by accident, Bob and Mallory found a card in the antique card catalogue at the library that suggested she had donated a copy of the book before her death."

"No, no," said Mr. Abelman. "That's impossible. I know about every Fedorov holding in the entire library."

"But this isn't a Fedorov holding," said Jupiter. "It's a Foderov holding. The card isn't there any more – it's been stolen – but when it was, it said that Jelena Orlova had donated an item connected to Foderov, V. Someone misspelled the name Fedorov."

"That *could* happen!" said Mr. Abelman, sounding a lot more excited. "Is it possible that a copy of Vadim's lost novel has been sitting under my nose for years now?"

"Not just possible, but almost a certainty," Jupiter said. "But Colton Clark may be on his way to the library right now to destroy it."

"Destroy it?" Mr. Abelman exploded. "Why would he do such a thing?"

"I don't have time to go into that at the moment," Jupiter said. "Where are you?"

"I'm at home," Mr. Abelman said.

"I think you should get over to the library and either try to apprehend them, or go up into the stacks and see if you can find something with the label Foderov, V. on it," Jupiter said. "We'll meet you there."

"Is Colton alone?" Mr. Abelman asked.

"No," Jupiter said. "He's got two other guys with him, and that guard who knows his father may be in on it too. He's working today."

"So that's his plan," Mr. Abelman said. "I never should have hired that son-of-a- ." He paused . "You'll get here soon, then?"

"Yes," Jupiter said. "But the three of us have to wait for Mallory. She and Cassandra were at Tracey Clark's house, which is why we even know about what's happening. As soon as they get here, we're on our way. If you get there first, hold them off, if you can."

"I certainly will," Mr. Abelman said. "See you shortly."

"Maybe we should call the police," Bob said.

"There's nothing they can do," Jupiter said. "If we tell them we think a crime is about to happen, they'll tell us they're sorry but to call back again after it's been committed."

Bob stood up and started pacing. "I wish we were there right now," he said.

"Me too!" Pete said. "Do you think Leif could drive us?"

"We have to wait for Mallory," Jupiter said. "Let me call her and make sure she's on her way."

He dialed her number on the landline and pressed the speakerphone button. The ringing seemed louder in the confines of Headquarters than it normally would have, and it went on and on, a frustrating number of times, before Mallory finally picked up.

"Mallory!" Jupiter said. "Why did it take you so long to answer? I was getting worried."

"The phone was in my pants pocket," Mallory explained, "and it was hard to get to. Why are you calling? Can you talk? I've been wanting to tell you the rest of what I've been thinking, but I knew you might be talking to Mr. Abelman."

"I wanted to make sure you were on the way," Jupiter said. "I just spoke to Cassandra's father, and he's meeting us at the library. How long until you get here?"

"Cassandra could drive for NASCAR," Mallory said. "She's a maniac. Still, as long as we're talking, anyway, I'd like to fill you in on the rest of what happened – and what I think is really going on."

"Please do," Jupiter said. "What did you find in Tracey Clark's house?"

"I found out from Colton's cousin – a really nice guy named Billy Davis – that when Ivan Ivanovich died, his house was jammed with stuff he'd collected and saved, and that most of it got sold with the property. Billy said a lot of it had come from Ivan Ivanovich's relative, who worked in the movies."

"In other words, Tracey Clark bought a lot of stuff that had belonged to Ivan Ivanovich," Jupiter said.

"Exactly," Mallory said. "And for almost nothing."

"Did you see any of it?" Jupiter asked.

"I didn't have much time to look," Mallory said. "But I found a lot of old movie posters hanging in the living room. I don't known whether Ivan Ivanovich had already framed them or if Tracey Clark framed them after she got them, but a good number of them are from movies that starred Fyodor Fedorov. And – get this – I also found a framed medal that seemed identical to the one Mr. Fedorov wore in that scene in *Dawn Over Petrograd.*"

"Do you think it was the medal the czar gave to Fyodor?" Jupiter asked.

"No," Mallory said. "I think it was a copy they made as a prop for the movie. Which makes me think that Ivan Ivanovich's relative was the prop man who helped Fyodor give clues about his real political sympathies in *Dawn Over Petrograd.* When the shoot was over, he gave the mock medal to his great-nephew."

"Who, as you learned," Jupiter said, "was a friend of Vadim's."

"We're getting close, guys. We just got to Rocky Beach," Mallory said. "Anyway, the real find was a stool with a needlepoint top. Tracey keeps it under her writing desk, and Billy Davis showed it to me. Ivan Ivanovich embroidered three things on it – a hammer and sickle, an American bald eagle, and the Cyrillic letters we've now grown familiar with – right next to the words *The Intemperate Imperium.*"

Bob had stopped his pacing and was staring at the phone. Pete was on his feet and looked like he was struggling to keep from shouting. Jupiter was flushed with heat, a sensation that started in his toes and seemed to shoot up his legs, through his torso, and into his brain.

"Anything else?" he asked Mallory.

"Billy said that there were piles of paper," Mallory said, "but I didn't see any. Tracey must have thrown them away a long time ago. Or carefully kept them."

Jupiter's voice was taut with tension. "Are you thinking what I'm thinking? he asked.

"You bet I am," Mallory said.

The clues had been there before him, but it was only now that he'd managed to put them all together. He could feel his blood pulsing in his fingertips. He felt fully alive.

"What if, as she was sifting through all the apparently valueless papers in Ivan Ivanovich's house, Tracey Clark found something that surprised her – a copy of Vadim Fedorov's lost novel? What if she started reading it and realized how good it was? What if she decided she'd simply steal it and pass it off as her own?" said Jupiter intently.

"It's the only thing that makes sense,"

Mallory said. "There's no other reason why Tracey would be offering to pay her brother to destroy the manuscript in the library unless she knew it was the evidence that would convict her of theft and plagiarism. And it would certainly explain why it seemed to everybody that her writing had suddenly gotten much, much better."

"But how did she think she could ever get away with it?" Bob said.

"She almost did, didn't she?" Jupiter said. "She was very clever. More clever than I would have given her credit for. Remember the writing process she outlined for us the night of Cassandra's book party, Mallory?"

"I do indeed," Mallory said. "She told us in such detail, and I found it very interesting."

"What process?" Bob wanted to know.

Why in the world had it taken him so long to figure out the connection between Tracey Clark and the missing novel? Jupiter wondered, as he explained.

"She writes on a computer, of course. And every day, after she finishes her work for the day – three or four pages or so – she duplicates the file. Then the next day she works in the new file, revising or writing new pages. At the end of that day, she duplicates that file and starts the process over the next day. She said she must have four hundred files, each one carefully dated by the computer, each one a little longer than the one before it."

"But all those days, in all those files, she wasn't writing," Mallory said. "She was typing. Each day she'd take out Vadim's manuscript and type out three or four new pages."

"Because Tracey Clark is certainly smart enough to realize that she would need to cover her tracks," Jupiter added. "If she simply planned to steal the work of a much better writer, then what better way to make it appear as though she'd written the book herself than to type just a little of the lost manuscript into a file every day for over a year so that she could supposedly prove afterwards that it had taken her that long to get it done? All the date stamps on the files would be there, in chronological order – to prove something that never happened!"

"That's really devious. And sickening," Bob said.

"It certainly is," Jupiter said. "It speaks of patience bordering on the pathological. Most thieves are more interested in immediate gratification – they generally use the smash-and-grab method. But Tracey Clark was biding her time – even dragging her writing group into the deception."

"You can say that again. I learned today that Tracey never shared any of her writing electronically, the way the other group members did," Mallory said. "She insisted on handing out copies on paper and on collecting them all afterwards. That way she kept any evidence of what she was doing strictly under her own control. But I outwitted her. I've got the pages she handed out in my pocket."

"Good work, Mallory!" Jupiter almost shouted.

"She also told us she kept audio files of herself," Mallory went on, "thinking out loud about what might happen next in the book. Pure fiction – a total act. The audio files, followed by the written files, would seem to provide convincing evidence to whoever might doubt it that she'd written the book herself."

"Unless," Jupiter said, "there was another copy of the book she was stealing somewhere else – like in the American Film History Library. I don't know when she found out about its existence, but when she did, it must have driven her crazy. Ever since, I'm sure she's been planning to destroy it. But she couldn't get to it because the stacks are restricted, and she couldn't ask to see it because then her name would be connected to it."

"Do you think she got her father to give public money to the library just to get that surly guard hired so she'd have a way to get to the manuscript?" Bob asked.

"I wouldn't put it past her," Jupiter said. "But I think our showing up on the scene may have induced her to push her plan forward."

"Yes," Mallory said. "I don't know what made her suspicious, but that Foderov card went missing after she saw us in the library. There's just one thing that bothers me."

"What's that?" Jupiter asked.

"Well, I'm not even sure we ever told you this, but when Bob and I were talking with Hector Sebastian, he told us that one night after a Mystery Writers' of America meeting, he and some other guys, including Vadim Fedorov, went to a bar where Vadim told him a story about a friend of his who was supposedly working on a novel written in the first person by a woman. Even though he denied it to Hector, it seems pretty clear that the supposed 'friend' was actually Vadim himself."

"Yes," Bob said. "I agree."

"But when I read the pages that Tracey submitted, I saw that the story was written in the third person, not the first person. *She* − not

I – did this and thought that."

"But in other respects?" Jupiter said.

"The character was a woman," Mallory confirmed, "who'd come to California after the Russian Revolution."

"I wouldn't worry very much about the first person/third person thing," Bob said. "I'm sure it's just one more attempt on Tracey's part to cover her tracks. I'm not totally sure, but I think it wouldn't be all that hard to take a first person voice and turn it into third person. All you'd have to do, really, is change the pronouns and then add a bit of explanation here and there. So Tracey wasn't just typing; she was also doing a kind of translation, from first person to third."

"That sounds about right," Jupiter said. "And it makes sense. She knew enough about her limitations as a writer to understand it would be one thing too many for people to believe she could write convincingly in the voice of a Russian woman much older than she was. So she distanced herself by changing the voice."

"Yes," Mallory said. "Very clever."

"Very clever, indeed," Jupiter said. "But ingenuity in the pursuit of evil is never admirable."

"We're here, Jupiter," Mallory said. "I

can see the Salvage Yard's gates."

"O.K.," Jupiter said. "See you immediately. Over and out." He punched the speakerphone off and said, "Let's go."

It was a bit of a scramble toward Easy Three as Jupiter, with Pete and Bob fast on his heels, made for the door. They flung it open and poured through just as the car, with Cassandra driving, screeched to a halt by the Office.

Jupiter ran by Mallory. "Just a minute. I have to tell Aunt Mathilda," he yelled as he clattered up the steps. Aunt Mathilda was sitting behind the office desk. She looked up, astonished. Uncle Titus was reading a magazine in a chair behind her.

"What in the name of all that's holy is going on?" Aunt Mathilda said, her voice rising. "Land sakes, Jupiter, you're all red in the face."

"That's probably true," Jupiter said. He certainly felt comprehensively agitated. "I just came to say that the four of us have to go right now. We're off to the film library in Boxwood."

"Right now?" Aunt Mathilda said, glancing at the clock on the wall. "Why, it's nearly seven o'clock! Have you had any dinner?"

"We grabbed a sandwich," Jupiter said. "I have to go."

"When will you be back?" Aunt Mathilda asked.

"As soon as possible," Jupiter said.

"Just a minute, young man," Uncle Titus said. "I have a puzzle – "

But Jupiter was already through the door and down the steps.

When he looked at Cassandra's car, he saw what a tight squeeze it would be for the five of them and he thought of suggesting they take the Flex. But Cassandra and Mallory were already in place, and every second was precious.

He gestured to Pete and Bob, and the three of them jammed themselves into the back seat of the small car, which vibrated with excitement. Cassandra threw the car into reverse, turned around, and roared off through the Salvage Yard gates.

Jupiter somehow found himself squished in the middle between Bob and Pete. Bob looked quite pleased with himself for getting the window. Jupiter knew he was tired of always being in the middle, and he could see why. It was extremely uncomfortable. At least in the Flex there was more room. He jiggled his shoulders, trying to find a position he could live with.

"Sit still," Bob said.

"The cavalry to the rescue!" Pete said.

"Let's hope we get there in time," Jupiter said as they headed off, at top speed, toward the film library and a gang of thugs!

13

In A Jam

They were about two miles from the library when the taillights of the cars ahead of them began to flash red – three lanes of sudden warning. The irritation Bob was already feeling began to intensify. He had a bad feeling about this.

Cassandra stepped on the brakes, slowing way down, until they were at a complete stop, bumper to bumper, on a long gently arching overpass in the maze of southern California's highways. Below them, another highway sent cars rushing to their destinations, while next to them, separated by a heavy guard rail, the lanes of traffic heading north sped on, pounding over the expansion joints in the pavement.

Every time a semi or even a large delivery truck passed, it sent vibrations across the overpass. They seemed to be filtering up through the car's tires, making everything hum and rattle and shake. Bob had been on edge before, but now he thought he'd jump out of his skin. The vibrations made his teeth ache.

256

"What's going on?" Pete asked, leaning his head out the window and craning to see if he could get a view of what was stopping them.

"There must be an accident up ahead," Cassandra said. "Hopefully nothing serious."

Of course it was serious, Bob thought. Anything that stopped them was serious. He felt incredibly frustrated but also inexplicably angry – angry at Cassandra, as though she'd caused the traffic jam and angry at his friends who jostled in their seats and grumbled but who did not seem to share his large-scale dismay.

"Can you drive on the shoulder or something?" Bob asked. Every now and then a car inched forward to their right.

"No!" Mallory said. "I hate it when people do that. It's worse than people shoving in line ahead of you at the grocery store or movie theater."

"Don't worry," Cassandra said. "I'm sure they'll get this cleared away in no time, and then we're only a few minutes from the library. Besides, my dad must be there by now. If I know him, he'll go right to the stacks and get the archive box with the manuscript – or whatever it is – and take it somewhere Colton won't find it, like his office."

"It's the manuscript," Mallory said. "I'm sure of it."

Bob was sure of it too.

"Could you call your father?" Bob asked anxiously. "We'd all feel better if we knew the manuscript was safe."

"Sure," Cassandra said. She took out her phone and dialed and then sat placidly, holding it against her face. Finally she put the phone down and ended the call. "He's not answering," she said. "But there are lots of reasons that might be the case."

Like what? Bob wondered.

A moving truck sped past on the other side of the overpass, and Bob could practically see the asphalt shake as the vibrations traveled across and into his jaw. It was so extreme he thought the whole overpass might come apart and they'd plummet to the highway below.

Bob couldn't help remembering all the other times he'd been stuck in traffic in California, the land of ten zillion cars. He remembered once when he'd been with his father in downtown L.A., and on the way home, the traffic had stopped dead, five lanes of traffic, a parking lot from here to eternity, with the sun beating down on the metal roofs and people running out of gas as they kept their engines on for the air conditioning.

It was a special kind of hell, Bob thought. You were on your way somewhere, at speed, and all of a sudden you were caught up short and the car's forward momentum was translated to your body which kept wanting to move forward but couldn't, and the waiting kept going on and on and you couldn't relax and people were leaning on their horns and getting out of their cars, shading their eyes to see if they could figure out what was going on, and some were even climbing up and standing on the roof to get a better vantage. Maybe he should do that.

If Cassandra was right that there was an accident up ahead on the far side of the overpass, who knew how long it would take to clear the highway? In the meantime, it was entirely possible that the evidence proving that Tracey Clark was planning to pass off Vadim Fedorov's work as her own was being destroyed. Bob had an impulse to open the door and start running.

At least, for once, he wasn't in the middle.

"I just can't believe," Cassandra said, "that Tracey thought she could get away with it. And even worse – that all of us in the writing

259

group believed her and praised her and didn't see what was right in front of us the whole time!"

Beside Bob, Jupiter cleared his throat. "I can see why you feel that way," he said, "but I hope at least you're glad about the good news."

"About Bob and Pete talking to people who were at the graduation party?" Cassandra said. "That's not good news. It's the *best* news!"

No, Bob thought. The best news was that Vadim Fedorov's manuscript had been found.

"Nothing's for sure, of course," Jupiter said, "until Colton Clark withdraws the threat of a lawsuit. But I'm almost certain that will happen when he's confronted with the evidence. We could search for the other people he jammed with that evening, but I don't think that will be necessary."

"Everyone remembers Ivan," Pete said. "They were all so happy to help. He must have been very popular."

"Particularly the evidence of the guy who remembered Ivan leaving the party early," Bob said. "Do you remember his name, Pete?"

"Lopez," Pete said. "Miguel Lopez."

"Do you know him, Cassandra?" Jupiter

asked.

"No," Cassandra said. "I didn't go to that high school."

"That's right," Jupiter said. "Anyway, from what Pete and Bob said about the specificity of his testimony – Ivan leaving before sunset – there's just no way that Colton can make a case. And there's other testimony to back Ivan up. I'm sure we can make this threat go away."

Bob knew Jupiter was trying to be reassuring, and was probably even trying to find a way to keep from being anxious himself, but at the moment, Bob found this chatter nothing but annoying. Why didn't Jupiter just stop talking? he wondered. He'd never been angry at Jupiter before, but he was angry now.

He zoned out as much as he could, closing his eyes and breathing deeply. Even so. he could feel that his hands had contracted into fists and he couldn't make them unclench.

Jupiter was talking now about the United States Copyright Office and the Library of Congress.

"This morning, I checked online to see if a book written by Vadim Fedorov was ever copyrighted in Washington," Jupiter said. "If Per Jorgensen was right that in the old days screenwriters like Vadim Fedorov always typed three copies of their screenplays, maybe he was also right that when Vadim Fedorov became Edison Ford, he might have kept the habit up.

"Since we now know – or think we know – that he gave both Jelena Orlova and Ivan Ivanovich a copy of his masterwork, maybe the third copy – the original, actually – was sent to the Copyright Office in Washington to be registered. But I couldn't find a record of it. Besides, it seems hugely unlikely that Vadim wouldn't have kept a copy of his book. But where could it have gotten to?" Jupiter said.

Bob shook his head in frustration. If Vadim had actually sent a copy of his book to the Copyright Office, and then left it to his grandson in his will, why hadn't he mentioned the copyright there? If Vadim had done that, none of this would have happened, and that Tracey Clark would never have been able – .

An image of her came into Bob's head – the way she'd looked at Cassandra's book party, as if butter wouldn't melt in her mouth, talking to Mallory and Jupe, and then yesterday at the library, talking to that guard and inviting Mallory to come to the writing group so Mallory could listen to "her" writing. The sheer gall of it was more than he could believe.

Ahead of them, brake lights were going off, and cars were beginning to inch forward. The lane next to them seemed to be moving just a bit more quickly, and Bob thought of asking Cassandra to merge over. But then the red lights all came back on, like a swarm of angry hornets, and they were stuck again. This traffic jam was making him crazy.

"How do you think Tracey Clark found out about the copy in the library in the first place?" Pete was asking.

"We can only surmise," Jupiter said. "But it seems likely that she came across the Foderov, V. card in the old card catalogue the same way Bob did – she was looking up Vadim and just flipped past his entries and found the odd card. Of course, she knew right away what she'd found. It must have been a shock."

"The name of the book was in both Russian and English on the footstool where she propped her feet every time she sat down to plagiarize," Mallory said.

"So even though the name in the card catalogue was only in Cyrillic, she knew for sure what it meant when she found it," Jupiter said. "Up until then, she'd thought she had the only copy. Now there was another one. And she knew that there'd be a paper trail if she asked a librarian to retrieve the manuscript and then she managed to steal it or destroy it."

Bob felt a sharp pain in his temple, as though he'd been stabbed. It faded quickly, but it had surprised him with its ferocity.

"But when?" Pete asked.

Jupiter shook his head. "Some time in the last weeks or months. She wasn't in a hurry at first."

"Ivan will be so flabbergasted when he hears all this," Cassandra said. "And so thankful. You guys are amazing."

He won't have anything to thank us for if Colton destroys the library copy, Bob thought. What was keeping the first responders? When would they get moving again?

"So how to get her hands on the manuscript?" Jupiter asked. "Mallory, I think you nailed it earlier."

"It was a complicated plan," Mallory said. "But it does make sense. First she convinced her father, who knows how, to give a taxpayer-funded grant to the library, and then she got him to get this thug a job. Undoubtedly he's a friend of Colton's, and he worked on her father's campaign, so it just seemed like a nice little piece of nepotism and didn't have an ulterior reason. All the while she was planning to use him to help her get to the manuscript."

Bob felt the rage rising inside him. "We've got to get there!" he exploded. "Damn it!"

Jupiter turned to him, concerned. "Bob, are you all right?" he asked. "You're not usually angry. Not like this."

"Well, I'm angry now," Bob said. "I'm angry at all this traffic. Only in California! And whoever was driving sloppily and got into an accident!"

"Calm down," Jupiter said. "There's nothing we can do about it. We'll get there as soon as we can."

He turned back to Cassandra. "We can't exactly prove any of this," he said, "at least not yet, that is, but all signs do indeed point to Tracey Clark getting an inside man on the job, and then getting her brother to act as muscle. She's a cool one. She's sitting back at her house, eating hamburgers by the pool, surrounded by witnesses who can swear that she was nowhere near the library at the time that someone broke in and stole a copy of something or other. And even if Colton was suspected, unless the guard or one of the other perps talked, there'd be no way to prove she didn't write the book if they managed to burn the only other copy."

"By the way," Mallory said to Cassandra. "I keep forgetting to ask you. What was the title that Tracey gave the book?"

"She's calling it *The Hotel California*," Cassandra said.

"She even stole the modern title!" Bob yelled. He hadn't thought that he could feel angrier, but now he did. He realized he wasn't angry at the traffic, or at Jupiter or Pete or Mallory or at the fact that they weren't as angry as he was. He was angry at Tracey Clark. He was furious. He was enraged.

He thought of the villains they'd run into recently – the pair who had kidnapped him and Pete and had taken them to Catalina Island; the forger and money-launderer who had held Pete at knifepoint; the ICE agent and Greek turncoat who had attempted to steal the treasures of ancient Greece and pin it on a meek Classics professor. But none of them held a candle to Tracey Clark.

And then he realized that the anger he felt was not his own alone. He was angry on behalf of Vadim Fedorov, a true artist who had built a career as a screenwriter only to have his life derailed when he was accused of being a Russian agent or spy or sympathizer.

He could only imagine the effect that act of aggression had had on Fedorov, and the way it would have shaken his faith in both America and his chosen community of Hollywood. But then he had started over and built not just a new but a fantastically successful life as Edison Ford, the mystery novelist.

And at the same time he was publishing an excellent mystery every year or so, he was also working on a long and serious novel which Bob assumed was wonderful and which, he thought, had to be – at least in part – about politics and writing and the way that governments should never be allowed to interfere with or dictate what writers write or how they decide to interpret history.

And then this dishonest, hypocritical, fraudulent, double-dealing, Janus-faced, and utterly spoiled young woman had found a manuscript of a book – whose pages she could never have imagined, much less written – in a house she'd just bought with the proceeds of an acrimonious divorce. Rather than give it to the writer's descendants, or make it public – rather than celebrate it or tell the world about it – she'd decided to steal it.

Bob thought back over the whole list of bad guys that he and Pete and Jupiter and

Mallory had run into, and he couldn't remember one who he had felt such a mixture of contempt and disgust for. He hadn't liked any of them, but most had been motivated by human emotions he was at least familiar with. They were greedy and wanted money and the things it could buy; they were envious or hurt and wanted to punish others.

But two had come close. He remembered the history professor, Daniel Hernández, who had concocted a letter supposedly written by Kit Carson that falsified the historical record and slandered a dead man. And the fraudulent German con man Günther Böhm who'd pretended to be an artist and who wanted to cut up a painting by Edvard Munch and use it in his so-called collages for the sake of publicity.

As semis streamed past in the other direction, the bridge continued to vibrate, and the cars in their ranked files continued to go nowhere – as the others in the car finally fell silent – Bob realized that Tracey Clark had something in common with Hernández and Böhm.

All three of them had tried to pass themselves off as respectable, respected, and educated members of society, when they'd been undermining the values of that society and lying to it. They'd been turning basic human values on their head. Hernández had committed forgery, fraud, and defamation of a man who wasn't alive any more; Böhm and Clark had committed a kind of fancy artistic theft, which also involved massive disrespect for the dead.

As Bob sat there, staring ahead at the taillights of the cars in front of them, an idea began to crystallize. There was really only one reason why he could be so angry, and that was because, without really knowing or understanding it, he identified with Vadim Fedorov.

Bob was a writer, too, and he took the theft of Vadim's novel personally. When he'd talked to Hector Sebastian, he'd been filled with admiration to consider that a friend of Vadim Fedorov who'd worked on a book for twenty years, had started the book over when he realized he was writing from the wrong point-of-view. He had to get it *right*.

Now he knew that the "friend" was really Vadim himself, and that his work on *The Intemperate Imperium* was the work of an unusually dedicated writer. Like the man who'd written the story "The Book and The Beast," he'd believed that writing something as well as you could write it was the most important thing in the world – and right now, Bob felt that both of those writers were right – and that if he became a writer himself, as he hoped to, they'd both be role models for his life.

Finally, something was happening up ahead. Bob couldn't see far, but it seemed that thousands of red taillights were blinking off, as people began to believe in the possibility of forward motion again. In the lane next to them, cars began to tug ahead.

In the heat of stasis, Bob had seen two young boys sitting hopelessly in the back seat of a Toyota, and now both of them were leaning into the front seat as if they were urging a sports team on.

One of them looked in Bob's direction, a huge grin on his face. Bob smiled and waved at him and the boy waved back. People did not like to be held captive, Bob thought. People valued freedom of movement as well as of thought.

"What's happening?" Pete asked.

"It looks like they've finally cleared a lane," Cassandra said. "We're merging."

It was almost – but not quite! – as frustrating as being stopped dead, the tantalizing stop-and-start of the lanes of cars as they jerked forward, as three lanes worked to become one. Cassandra put her blinker on and nosed the car toward the lane she wanted to join. Now the question was whether someone would let her in or whether she'd have to be aggressive.

"Go for it!" Pete said, and Bob agreed, but then the car inching up on their left stopped and Bob could see the driver, a young woman, motioning with her hand for Cassandra to move over.

"Thank you!" Cassandra said fervently, as she and Bob waved to the woman.

To the right, the lines of cars had also begun moving, not forward but toward them, and even now, when Cassandra had managed to join the moving lane, it was slow going as everyone began to allow a car to join the procession.

It was at least another five minutes before they began to move at steady speed, only a few miles an hour but far better than standing still. A couple of hundred yards later they came upon the reason for the backup – a car with a family of four had broken down in the middle lane, and when a car in the right lane had slowed down, the car behind had run into them. The highway was bright with pink flares and shards of broken glass.

It was only a minor accident and no one seemed to have been hurt. Still, there were four police cars on the scene and a tow truck and an ambulance. The three cars had been pulled to the side of the highway, but only one lane was moving. A policeman in a fluorescent yellow jacket was making sweeping motions with his arms, orchestrating a merge to get the cars in front past the accident scene.

Finally they were free of the entire mess and the highway opened up before them. The sense of space, the rush of air through the open windows was exhilarating, and Bob was once again astounded at how quickly the sense of entrapment dissipated. It was almost as though it hadn't happened. He felt lighter – but he still felt angry, and he knew that feeling wouldn't go away any time soon.

Around him everyone started talking, as relieved as he was to be headed toward the library again, to have a goal in mind – rescuing the long-lost manuscript before it could be burned.

"How far are we?" Bob asked.

"About a mile and a half," Cassandra said. "We get off the highway at the next exit and then we've got some city streets to contend with." There were traffic lights and pedestrians jaywalking and some congested traffic as well. *Come on come on come on*, Bob thought. The library was actually only about twenty minutes from Rocky Beach, on a good day, but it had been almost twice as long since they'd left the Salvage Yard, and the sun was setting.

At last they broke away from the downtown area and came to the outskirts, where the imposing library had been built on a rise overlooking the valley. The arc lights had come on, revealing an empty parking lot – or almost empty. As Cassandra pulled as close to the building's entrance as possible, Bob saw three cars.

"There's my father's car," Cassandra said.

"And that's the car I saw at Tracey Clark's," Mallory said. "That means Colton and the others are already here!"

Bob's heart was hammering in his chest. The bad guys had gotten there first, but maybe they'd been thwarted by Mr. Abelman. Maybe the manuscript was safe. The five of them poured out of Cassandra's car and started running. As they dashed past the third car, Bob noticed a parking sticker on the driver's side of the windshield, up by the visor. American Film History Library STAFF, it said, in red letters.

The security guard's car.

The library was dark and quiet. To Bob, the long series of granite steps leading to the entrance seemed steeper in the gathering dusk.

"I hope Mr. Abelman is all right," Jupiter said, huffing a bit as they neared the top. "If he can't meet us, how are we going to get into the library at all?"

They clustered together at the main door. Bob peered through the glass at the entrance, shading his eyes, but the inside was too murky, and he couldn't make anything out.

Jupiter pulled on the door handle hard, as if he expected it to be locked, but it opened easily. Either Mr. Abelman or the guard had left it unlocked, Bob thought.

Quietly they filed inside. It was spooky, with no lights. The air seemed dense. In the far back Bob could see the faint orange dots of security lights, like glowing embers. The potted trees sent their branches high into the atrium and the tangled web helped block any residual light from the skylights. They stood trying to get their bearings, letting their eyes adjust.

"What's that?" Pete asked, alarmed.

From somewhere, weird creepy music streamed, faint but unmistakable.

14

Pete Mops Up

The music raised the hair on the back of Pete's neck. It sounded like an organ and reminded him of the Blue Phantom and Terror Castle. He'd expected four thugs and a run for a manuscript, not a haunted library. He glanced at his friends, all of whom looked confounded and uncertain.

For a moment the five of them stood rooted to the spot. It was creepy in the atrium, its darkness strafed by the occasional flash of headlights from the road that ran below the library's parking lot. Beside him, Bob looked fierce and tense, his hands clenched into fists. At least Pete wasn't angry, not the way Bob was. He was grateful for that. Anger kept you from thinking straight, and Pete wanted to be thinking straight.

He'd been frustrated by the long wait in traffic. In fact, he'd been frustrated by this entire case, which had jumped around from one problem – Colton Clark threatening Ivan – to another – the missing novel. He'd been thrilled to have Per Jorgensen appear so suddenly, but also bothered by what seemed to him to be his own inability to contribute anything of genuine value, so he was glad that some solid action had broken out.

Pete was good at action, he thought, and most of the timidity of his earlier years was gone. He hadn't conquered his fears, exactly, but he'd learned to face them. That, he'd come to understand, was the true meaning of bravery. He didn't know what lay ahead. Maybe they'd get the manuscript without any trouble, but if there was trouble, he knew he'd have to take the lead. He was the biggest, strongest person present.

Still, as strong and fit as Pete was – and even with Jupe and Bob as backup – he was a little worried that if it came to a physical confrontation, they'd have a hard time winning it. After all, it would be them against Colton Clark, his two thug friends, and the security guard. They were all in their twenties, or older, and the guard, after all, had gotten the job not only because he knew Colton's father but because he was in good physical shape and no doubt had had training in taking down opponents. The four thugs might be too much for the four of them.

And where was Mr. Abelman?

Suddenly someone was screaming – a high-pitched bloodcurdling scream that trailed off into silence. Pete couldn't tell whether it was a man or a woman. Adrenaline coursed through him. It had come from the screening room off to the right. No one else moved until Pete stepped forward and opened the door.

The music was much louder now, the high shrieks of violins, the rumble of tympani. On the screen, black and white images played. A woman was running, tripping, falling. Someone was behind her, a hooded man with a knife. The screams had come from a movie, and the music was its soundtrack. What was it doing on when the library was closed?

In the flickering light from the screen, Pete saw a figure hunched over at the end of the last row. He and the others ran over to find Mr. Abelman, gagged and tied to the seat. Blood ran from a gash on the back of his head. The thugs had knocked him out, then dragged him into the screening room, lashed him to a chair, and turned on a movie.

Cassandra knelt by her father's side as Jupiter took out his Swiss Army knife and cut him free. Cassandra looked very pale in the light from the screen.

"Dad," she said, "Dad. Talk to me."

She cupped his cheek with her hand.

At her touch, Mr. Abelman seemed to regain consciousness.

"Cassandra?" he mumbled. "Oh, my head." He winced.

"What happened, sir?" Pete asked.

Mr. Abelman turned, trying to make eye contact, and groaned. "I – I don't really know. I was walking down the hall, on my way to the stacks, when someone hit me from behind."

His eyes rolled and he slipped back into unconsciousness.

"I should call an ambulance," Cassandra said. "And the police."

"That's a very good idea," Jupiter said. "A crime has certainly been committed now."

Cassandra stayed with her father, but Pete, Bob, Jupiter, and Mallory ran out of the theater and back into the atrium. By now it was fully dark outside – a wave of black velvet beyond the glass walls of the museum. The parking lot shone hotly under the pooled light of the arc lamps, and beyond it, Pete could see the headlights of cars, like tiny illuminated insects, scurrying along the lines of highways.

The library was even darker now, except for the steady orange glow of the few scattered emergency lights. As the four of them approached the library's Circulation Desk, Pete looked up at the restricted stacks above. Four lights bobbed, four flashlights whose beams careened here and there, slicing the darkness. That was where the thugs were!

He noticed that one of the two glass elevators had stopped on the third floor – the higher of the two restricted stacks – while the other one was where they both should have been, to the side of the long sinuous Circulation Desk, and wide open.

"Look," Pete said in an urgent whisper, pointing. "They're up there. The guard's with them; there are four of them. And they took the elevator up. If they all come down at once, how are we going to stop them? They're older and bigger than we are and probably a lot more used to fighting."

"We can't take the other elevator up," Bob said, "because then we can't keep our eyes on them, and we can't wait for them to come down."

"I agree," said Jupiter.

"There has to be another way to get up there," Pete said. "Isn't there a law about emergency exits and fire stairs? I'll go looking. The three of you stay here and guard the elevators. Cassandra must have called the police by now. I'm sure they'll get here before Colton and his friends try to leave."

Pete wasn't sure, but he wanted to sound positive.

"I don't want you to go alone, Pete," Jupiter said. "You may need help, or someone who can go for help."

"I'll go," Bob said. "I want to. I couldn't be more angry about what these guys are trying to get away with."

There was a utility closet off the atrium, and Pete walked over and pulled open the door, looking for anything that could be used as a weapon, anything that might even the fight. In the corner, three rag mops with metal handles leaned against the wall. Bingo! In one hand Pete grabbed the mops, and in the other a galvanized metal bucket. The cotton mop heads were damp, and a little heavy. But it was the handles he was interested in.

He ran back to his friends and gave one of the mops to Jupiter and one to Bob.

"If you need to clean the floor with someone," Pete said, "do it with these."

He glanced up at the stacks where the flashlight beams continued to punch through the darkness. The thugs had assaulted Mr. Abelman before he'd had a chance to say anything, so there was no way he'd told them that Pete and the others were coming. This gave the four of them the advantage of surprise. They had no reason to think that their presence had been noted. The Three Investigators didn't have flashlights of their own, the library was dark, and they'd been very quiet. The thugs wouldn't suspect anyone else was on to them.

"Come on, Bob," Pete whispered. Bob grabbed his mop and started to follow Pete.

"Wait," Mallory said. She dashed behind the Circulation Desk, grabbed something fastened to a post, and returned with what Pete could now see was a squat red fire extinguisher.

"If the thieves make it down in the elevator," she said, "maybe I can stop them by spraying this in their faces."

"Great idea!" Pete said. "Then Jupiter can mop *that* up!"

Pete didn't know why he was saying all these ridiculous things, but for some strange reason he actually almost felt like laughing.

He motioned to Bob, put his finger to his lips, and then began jogging toward a hallway in the back of the building that he and the others hadn't been down before. The hallway was murky, lit only by the bulb in an EXIT sign about halfway down the hall. They passed the doors of what Pete supposed were offices.

"Do you know where you're going?" Bob whispered.

"No," Pete said. "I'm just keeping my fingers crossed."

The EXIT sign was above a door that opened onto an interior courtyard. It was pitch black out there and Pete could see nothing. But not far from it was another set of metal doors. Each of them had a rectangular pane of safety glass with embedded wire mesh, and each of them said FIRE DOOR. KEEP CLOSED. Behind the doors was a large tiled landing and a flight of stairs leading down to the basement and up to the restricted stacks. The staircase was sufficiently out of the way of the library's patrons so that no one would be wandering up it, trying to gain access to the restricted areas without permission.

Pete grinned at Bob, held the door open so that Bob could get through, and then slipped through himself. Carrying his mop and bucket, he started up the stairs, Bob close behind him holding the mop handle in two hands like a staff. They passed the door leading to the second floor of stacks and continued up to where Pete had seen the flashlights.

There was a wire mesh window in the door at the top of the stairs as well, and Pete peered through it. He glimpsed a flash of light but didn't see anybody. The thugs were several rows away from them. Bob eased open the door and he and Pete slipped through as soundlessly as possible, closing the door gently behind them. Surprise would be their greatest ally, Pete knew.

They paused for a minute while Pete breathed deeply, to slow his heart down and to calm himself. When he was ready, he gestured with his head and started creeping toward the aisle where the thugs were operating. They were talking quietly, cowed by the size of the place and the darkness, and Pete couldn't make out what they were saying.

He paused at the end of the stacks, his back against the metal support. Then as carefully as he could, he craned his neck and peered around the corner. In the flashlights' glow, he was able to get a good look at two of them – Colton and one of his thug friends, who was holding a dark gray archive box. As he planned his move, another of the thugs spotted him and called out in a piercing whisper, "Guys! We've got trouble!"

Though he was dismayed at being spotted, the comment gave Pete an unexpected boost. He certainly hoped he really *was* trouble.

Without time to plan his attack, Pete started yelling as he rushed toward the guy who had seen him, the pail hanging from his wrist, the mop handle secure in both hands. He took a swipe at him with the mop, but the narrow space between the stacks prevented him from getting any leverage. He decided to use the metal handle as a spear, but the guy side-stepped, and Pete had put so much force into the thrust that it flew out of his hands and went sliding down the aisle into the darkness.

The guy lunged forward, and this time Pete grabbed the bucket, swung from behind him, over his shoulder, and hit the guy square on the top of the head. He went down in a heap and stayed there. He wasn't moving.

Behind him, Pete heard a commotion and he turned in time to see the surly security guard attack Bob. Bob had time to use his mop, and he smacked the guy in the ribs. This knocked him sideways but not out, and for a moment he stood there with his hands on his hips smirking.

"Is that the best you can do, you little punk?" the guard said. "I've seen third-grade girls stronger than you."

Uncertainly, Bob looked back at Pete, who was flooded with rage on Bob's behalf. He dropped the bucket and strode past until he was several feet in front of the guard.

"Oh, here's the big man to the rescue," the guard said. He raised his hands and wiggled them. "Whew, I'm scared!" he said in a high tremulous voice.

"You ought to be," Pete said. Without thinking, he leaped forward and head-butted the guard, smashing him in the nose with his forehead. The guard staggered backwards, his hands to his face, as he tried to regain his footing. His nose was bleeding badly. His eyes crossed, he fell to his knees and then toppled to the floor, out cold.

Pete laughed out loud. Two down, he thought. Two to go.

He'd headed lots of balls in soccer before, rising into the air to meet them on their downward arcs, but he'd never head-butted anyone. It hurt much less than he had thought it would. The trick had been to use the hard bony part of his head – his forehead – against a softer part of the opponent's face.

From behind him, Colton and his other friend rushed past, like broken field runners, shoving first Bob and then Pete out of the way, jumping over the guard's body. Colton was carrying the manuscript box. Before Pete could regain his balance and get to them, they'd raced to the elevator and hit the DOWN button. The elevator doors began closing.

Pete rushed to the railing and stared down into the atrium as the glass elevator descended. "Jupe! Mallory!" he called. "It's Colton and one other guy. They're coming. Get ready. Colton's got the book!"

"I can't get the fire extinguisher to work!" Mallory called back, her voice agitated.

"Do you still have the mop, Jupe?" Pete asked.

"Yes," Jupiter said.

"Use it!" Pete yelled.

From above, the action that followed looked like a weird video game. Colton and his thug friend rushed out and stopped short, casing the situation. Mallory was frantically trying to pull a plastic pin out of the fire extinguisher's handle. Jupiter swung the mop low to the ground as Colton and his friend suddenly charged past. His swing was fast and accurate and it picked up force as it continued its arc.

He hit both the thieves in the shins, and they went down as though they were stalks of wheat and he was swinging a scythe. Colton was sent sprawling. The archive box he was carrying flew from his arms as he braced to soften his fall, and it hit the tiled floor of the atrium and burst open, sending pages of the manuscript flying all over.

Jupiter ran to gather them together, but Colton had scrambled to his feet and beat him to it, shoving him so hard that he sat down heavily. Colton grabbed a bunch of pages and brandished them.

"At least I can burn *some* of it," he snarled as he took a silver cigarette lighter out of his pocket, flipped open the lid, and struck a flame. He'd managed to light one corner of the pages on fire when he was hit with a swoosh of white foam.

He dropped the pages instantly and tried to cover his face, but it was too late. Mallory had jimmied loose the pin that kept the fire extinguisher from accidentally discharging, and now she was wielding it like a spray gun. She directed the nozzle first at Colton and then at his friend, covering their faces and shoulders with a thick coat of foam.

From above, as he watched the whole thing, Pete whooped.

"Come on, Bob," he yelled. "Let's go down."

With Bob close behind, Pete raced back to the fire stairs and down them at top speed. He ran down the hallway and into the atrium just in time to see Colton Clark and the other thug slipping and sliding on the foam but somehow managing to make it across the tiled floor toward the entrance doors. Pete heard police sirens and watched as two cruisers, their red and blue emergency lights flashing, careened into the library's parking lot. Their headlights illuminated the fleeing figures of Colton Clark and his friend.

As if transfixed by the lights, Colton stopped short and threw his hands into the air while his friend made a run for the darkness. But the second cruiser followed and caught him before he'd gotten too far.

An ambulance had followed them and now drove up to the library's entrance, and two white-coated EMTs jumped out.

"Hey, guys," Bob yelled. "You should have seen Pete! He head-butted the guard! He went down like a ton – like a ton of corrupt security guard!"

Jupiter and Mallory were on their hands and knees on the floor, gathering the pages that had become airborne when Colton had fumbled the box. Jupiter looked up, agitated but smiling.

"Well done, Pete!" he said. "We were right that you're a bighorn sheep in disguise."

Pete hadn't thought of that! In the chimera logo he'd had Connor O'Malley design for The Three Investigators, Jupiter was a golden eagle, Bob was a bobcat, and he was a bighorn sheep. He'd originally resisted that last connection, but right now, it seemed totally appropriate.

"Come help us," Mallory called. "The manuscript went everywhere."

"Is it all here?" Bob asked anxiously.

"We won't know," Mallory said, "until we've gathered all the pages."

Pete and Bob rushed to help them.

Mallory had picked up the archive box that had held the pages and put it to the side. As Pete examined it, he saw it was made of heavy dark gray cardboard, like all the others that had lined the shelves on the floor where he and Bob had apprehended the burglars. It had a flip top that had opened as it had flown through the air, releasing its contents.

The box looked pristine to Pete, its edges crisp and clean, no signs of wear anywhere on it, as though it had not been taken down and examined since it had first been put in the stacks. On the spine that would have faced outward on the shelf, as well as on the front, were rectangular white stickers on which had been typed FODEROV, V. and the title in Cyrillic.

Pete shook his head. What a lot of confusion and trouble had been caused by the transposition of two letters. He saw that, while it might have originally been a typing mistake, it had been repeated on both tags as well as on the card for the library's original catalogue. He hadn't seen the digital catalogue, but he was sure the author's name appeared in the same form there as well. He resolved to remind himself that there was no such thing as a little mistake.

He turned back to helping Jupiter and Mallory with the pages.

"They're all out of order," Mallory said.

"Yes," Jupiter said, "but at least they're numbered. We should each take a bunch of the pages and put them in numerical order. We can collate them later when we put the whole manuscript back together."

Pete took his pile and sat on the floor organizing them. The manuscript was a bit blurry, and he realized he was holding a carbon copy, just as Per had suggested. He wiped his thumb across a word, and it smeared easily. He let his eye fall from time to time on a paragraph or a sentence of text. The writing was very sophisticated, he thought, filled with detailed descriptions and occasional pages of dialogue that seemed like political discussions. They were all, of course, in English.

"What's the page in a manuscript called that has the book's title on it?" he asked.

"You mean the title page?" Bob asked, grinning.

Pete started laughing. "Yeah. The title page. Has anyone found it yet?"

No one had.

"We're looking for it," Mallory said. "It has to be somewhere."

The EMTs, followed by a policeman, came up the library's steps and entered the atrium. Pete saw that Mr. Abelman had staggered out of the screening room and was standing shakily on his feet. Cassandra was with him, holding onto his elbow. She must have turned the movie off; Pete could no longer hear the music that had added a strange and unnerving element to the evening.

After the EMTs did a quick check of her father, Cassandra gestured to the armchairs arranged under the potted trees and helped

Mr. Abelman over to them. The policeman followed them, sat down, and took out a notepad. Clearly, Pete saw, he would be taking notes as Mr. Abelman explained what had happened.

Soon the policeman would come over and talk to them, Pete thought.

He turned back to his stack of pages and finished putting them in order. There were large gaps in the numbers, but he could only assume that the pages missing from his stack were in Mallory's, Bob's, or Jupiter's.

"O.K.," Bob said. "Give your stacks to me and I'll put them all together." Pete got up and stretched, flexing his back, which was a little stiff from having sat bent over.

Bob worked quickly − so quickly that he had the manuscript all together in no time.

"It's almost all here," Bob reported. "The corner of page 121 is burnt, and a bunch of pages are wet from the fire extinguisher, but it looks pretty good."

"Almost all here?" Pete asked.

"There's no title page," Bob said.

"Oh no!" Mallory said. "Without it, we won't know for sure what English title Vadim chose for it. We *think* we know, but Ivan Ivanovich could have translated the Russian differently."

Everyone was puzzled until Jupiter said, "Wait a minute! What's that?"

Pete turned in the direction Jupiter was pointing. A single sheet of paper had somehow skidded and slipped under the Circulation Desk, and Jupiter's eagle eye had seen it.

"I'll get it," Pete said. He was already on his feet and he dashed over and lay prone on the floor, fishing under the desk until his fingers touched the single piece of paper. He caught it by the edge and pulled it out.

It was the novel's title page. A thrill ran up his spine.

He jumped to his feet and turned to his friends who were looking at him expectantly.

"Hey, guys," he yelled. "It says what we thought it would! Well, almost! It actually says *The Unbridled Empire: A Writer's Story*. And it's not by Vadim Fedorov, but Edison Ford!"

15

The Indefatigable Ink

Jupiter stood on a small stepladder in his living room, an electric drill in his hand. His shoulder ached but the job was almost finished. For days he'd avoided putting up Aunt Mathilda's new curtain rods, but that morning she'd cornered him and made him promise. As soon as this last bracket was fastened, he could put the rods in place, and then Aunt Mathilda could hang her new curtains whenever she wanted to. With his left hand he steadied the bracket. With the other, he pulled the trigger and drove the last screw home.

It had been three days since the melee at the American Film History Library and the successful recovery of the lost Vadim Fedorov novel. As Jupiter thought back on what had happened, he was pleased to remember what a group effort it had been. They were a very good team, and having Mallory as a full-time member was working out remarkably well.

She'd made major contributions to all three cases this summer, and she had a wicked trigger finger with a fire extinguisher, not to

mention a remarkable record of going under-
cover. He thought it was great that she was
going to be designing a new Three Investigators' headquarters – and that she'd had the
idea to call the new one HQ2, and the old one
HQ1.

It was funny how much it mattered what
you called something, Jupiter thought. In a few
days, he and the others, along with Worthington and Califia, would be going to the world
premiere of Daman's *Time Twist* sequel and
then to the party at the producer's house. Califia had played opposite Daman Duwalia as Juliet at the Rocky Beach Summer Theatre festi-
val the year before, and Jupiter remembered
Califia reciting the famous Shakespeare line
that a rose by any other name would smell as
sweet.

At the time, he hadn't thought much
about it, but he was thinking about it now. It
was certainly a memorable line, but was it
true? Had Vadim Fedorov been exactly the
same human being he'd been after he'd
adopted the *nom de plume* Edison Ford? Had
Pete's grandparents felt any different about
themselves after they changed their surname
from Crespillo to Crenshaw when they left
Mexico and came to America? Had the fact

that his parents had named him Jupiter shaped him as he'd been growing up?

Jupiter also found himself wondering whether Vadim Fedorov would have written a slightly different novel based on his parents' experience of leaving Russia and coming to America if the title he'd chosen for it had been different. After all, even though Mr. Abelman – who was home now from the hospital – had confirmed that *The Intemperate Imperium* was an accurate translation of the prop in *Dawn Over Petrograd*, in the end, Vadim had decided to call his novel *The Unbridled Empire* instead. Jupiter guessed that, to its writer, the title must have seemed more American, and therefore more compelling. Also, the title *Intemperate Imperium* was a bit redundant, Jupiter thought; by definition, if it was an empire, it was into power over others.

To his dismay, when he'd been biking down Main Street the day before, he'd seen a banner poster announcing a *Going Out Of Business Sale* in the window of Miles Hardware. He'd jammed on his brakes, parked, and run into the store to ask Mr. Szabó if it was really true.

Mr. Szabó had nodded sadly, and all that Jupiter had been able to do was sympathize when the man said it wasn't just the competition from online businesses that had made it impossible to go on. It was even more the politicians and bureaucrats and lifetime appointees who thought they were entitled to make the rules for everyone. He'd implied again what he'd implied the day Jupiter had met Mrs. Vasiliev — that the best government is always the government that does the least amount possible to interfere with people's lives — and he'd actually said that he hoped America wasn't turning into just another ugly empire.

Ever since, Jupiter had been wondering about that — why Per Jorgensen had said he was going to direct a movie about the Viking empire. Per had invited Cassandra and Ivan, Mrs. Vasiliev, and Mallory and The Three Investigators to his house for a cookout that evening, to celebrate the fact that the director of *The Golden Age* had approved the final score for the movie, with Ivan's music in it. Jupiter supposed he could ask Per then.

Having finished putting up the brackets, Jupiter made short work of putting up the curtain rods themselves. His aunt had cut them all to the proper length, and they fit easily into their brackets. He decided not to screw the decorative finials to their ends; if he did, his aunt would have to unscrew them all to slip on the curtains. When he was done, he stood back and surveyed his work with satisfaction, then put his uncle's drill away in its case and collapsed the folding stepladder.

In a little while Pete and Bob would be arriving for their case debriefing, and Mallory was already here – working in the shed that had become her favorite. Then Ivan and Cassandra would pick the four of them up and take them out to Per's – but before they arrived, he and the others should have some time to talk.

One thing they didn't need to talk about was the fact that Colton Clark's arrest had brought him to his senses; Ivan's lawyer had heard from Colton's lawyer that he wouldn't be proceeding with his lawsuit.

Jupiter put the furniture he'd moved back into place and tidied up the living room. Then he left the house and started toward the Salvage Yard. On the way, he noticed that three boards in the tall palisade fence surrounding the place were cracked and broken; he made a note to mention this to Leif and Magnus. Surely they could take the time to replace them. And the mural that local artists had painted around the entire perimeter of the fence needed sprucing up. That might have to wait for another summer.

He let himself through the gate and began walking toward the shed which Mallory had made her unofficial center of operations. As Jupiter approached it, he heard a commotion out in the street, beyond the wrought-iron gates of the Salvage Yard. It was Bob and Pete, arriving together on their bikes. They were in high spirits, whooping and yodeling and yelling to one another. The noise drew Mallory out of the shed, and she was standing beside him when their two friends skidded to a halt in the gravel. Pete was grinning madly and Bob was red-cheeked and breathing hard.

"I won!" Pete crowed.

"You did not!" Bob said. "Anyone could see I beat you."

As Pete took off his helmet, blue with black racing stripes, Jupiter smiled, remembering the helmet he'd worn for years, painted to look like a shark with grinning teeth.

Bob's helmet was bright green. Blue and green were also their chalk colors for leaving messages. Jupiter's color was red. He'd changed it from white not that long ago because white chalk was everywhere. Red, blue, and green were also the colors of ink that Jupiter's, Pete's, and Bob's names and titles were printed in on The Three Investigators' business cards.

Which made him think — especially with Mallory standing beside him, waving at the new arrivals. At some point in the not-too-distant future, The Three Investigators would need to print more copies of their card, and when they did, Jupiter thought Mallory's name should be included as The Three Investigators' Special Consultant. Mallory didn't have a color of her own yet, and Jupiter wondered what she'd want if she could choose.

He looked at the shirt she was wearing today — a deep rich blue-green she called teal — and realized that it was probably her favorite color. Maybe that would be what she chose when the time came. They'd have to get her a new bike helmet, too, Jupiter thought.

Pete and Bob had parked their bikes and had cooled down a bit from their friendly competition. Bob wiped his palm across his forehead where sweat was still gathering, and then the four of them trooped into the shed where Mallory had been working.

Mallory had opened all the windows, and a breeze blew through, aided by a rotating fan at one end of the building, making the shed pleasantly cool. They all got drinks and settled in, but for some reason none of them felt like talking about the case just then. Or at least none of them but Jupiter.

What *they* felt like talking about was Per Jorgensen and how fantastic it was that he'd asked them to a cookout at his house that evening. Pete kept saying he couldn't believe their good fortune – that they were going to Per's today, and in just a few more days they'd also be going to the premiere of Daman Duwalia's new movie, with a Fourth of July party afterwards!

As for Mallory, she kept saying how much she liked fireworks – that if anything could make a big Hollywood party worth going to, it would be fireworks.

However, Bob finally turned to the case by saying that ever since they'd rescued Vadim's novel from the fire at the American Film History Library, he'd been calling Jason Abelman once a day to see if he had found out anything from the United States Copyright Office; he'd volunteered to do this when he heard about Jupiter's online research, and how it had come up empty.

"And has he?" asked Jupiter.

"Not really," Bob said. "He thinks they're going to assign the case to someone who'll have the authority to do a thorough search of the records from the months just before Vadim died to see if they can find a copy of the novel and a registration number. It's too bad I'm going to have to call the case *The Mystery of the Intemperate Imperium*," he added, "because I actually like Vadim's title better. *The Unbridled Empire: A Writer's Story* sounds more modern. It also makes it easier to understand that what Vadim was getting at was that empires and writers don't mix very well! That, in the end, empires turn on their own artists. I wish I could think of another title that had something to do with the case."

Bob's wish made Jupiter remember what his uncle had said, not long before, about the "immutable ideal" America had been founded on. For a moment, he thought of suggesting the phrase to Bob as a possible alternate title, but then decided that it wouldn't mean the same thing to Bob that it did to him.

"Speaking of empires and writers, it's incredible that by the time the police got to Tracey Clark's house, she'd already burned the copy of Vadim's book she'd found among Ivan Ivanovich's papers," Mallory said.

The others all nodded. The police had found a pile of ash in Tracey Clark's fireplace which had contained fragments of pages that looked like old manuscript paper. It seemed that the moment she'd found out her brother had been arrested, she'd gotten rid of the manuscript and wiped all her computer and audio files clean. By the time the police got a warrant, the evidence was gone.

Except for the evidence in Mallory's pocket, Jupiter thought. Although Tracey Clark had very cleverly never sent any pages of the book electronically to members of her writing group, and she tried to maintain total control by collecting the hard copies she handed out, Mallory had, effectively, outfoxed her.

But when Jupiter pointed that out, Mallory shook her head gloomily.

"A fat lot of good that did," she said. "When I gave the Boxwood police the pages I'd saved, they said fraud would be very hard to prove – partly because Tracey never made a penny from what she did, and the public never heard about it and in a fraud case you have to prove damages.

"But you know, I've been thinking of a title that might work for this case quite well. When I was doing some online research about Vadim Fedorov, I found an article by a scholar who'd read all his screenplays and novels, and who really, really admired him. He didn't seem to have ever heard the rumor that Vadim had written a literary novel, but even so, he clearly wished he had. He said he was a really good writer, with a good mind and soul, and what he called 'indefatigable ink.'"

"Wow!" said Bob. "I love that!"

"I did, too," said Mallory. "And I happen to know that six ships of the Royal Navy have been named H.M.S. *Indefatigable*. It's a great name for a ship, but I like it for ink, as well."

"But what does indefatigable mean, exactly?" Pete asked.

"It just means keeping on going and going, long after everyone else has gotten tired," Mallory said. "Relentless, I guess. Just keeping on with the job until it's done."

"And the job in this case is writing," Bob said. "Which is what was really so impressive about Ivan's grandfather. That when he was told he couldn't write screenplays any longer, he started a whole new career writing novels. And all the time he was writing the novels the public knew about, he was also writing a novel they didn't."

Just then, Jupiter and the others heard the sound of a car on gravel, and the four of them went out to greet Cassandra and Ivan and Mrs. Vasiliev. All three seemed in very good spirits, and although Ivan was driving the van from which Colton's thug friend had tried to steal a guitar, he'd cleared his equipment out of it and put in seats enough for all of them. Mrs. Vasiliev had brought a Fourth of July cake as a thank you to the Three Investigators for solving Ivan's case. It was big and flat, and iced with a big American flag, and Mrs. Vasiliev insisted on carrying it into the shed The Three Investigators had just left, for them to celebrate with on the Fourth.

Cassandra and Ivan had also brought gifts. Although Jupiter couldn't remember anyone ever mentioning to them The Three Investigators' custom of keeping mementos of their cases, it somehow didn't surprise him when Ivan handed him a carefully wrapped box and said, "Since you're the First Investigator, you should unwrap this. But it's really for all four of you. A remembrance of a memorable case. I've just started to read the novel, and although I have no idea if anyone will ever publish it, I think it's wonderful."

Tearing the paper off, Jupiter saw the archive box from the library – the one that had held Vadim's novel, with its original misspelled label.

"Open it," Ivan said. Jupiter flipped the top and found a clean copy of the long-lost novel inside it, along with a card that had clearly been torn from an old card catalogue – the card Mallory and Bob had seen at the Library of American Film History before it was stolen.

"Where did this come from?" he asked, holding it up for the others to see.

"Ms. Rodriguez found it on the floor of the stacks near where Pete head-butted the guard," Cassandra said. "Tracey Clark must have given it to Colton, and the thugs must have carried it to the library with them so that they could match the information on the card with the information on the archive box. Ms. Rodriguez offered us the box and the card as mementos of the occasion, but we thought they should go to you."

As Pete and Bob both started to talk at once about how much they liked to keep mementos, Cassandra reached for the long cardboard tube she was carrying and handed it to Mallory. Mallory took off the bow, reached into the tube, and pulled out what Jupiter saw was an architectural plan.

"It's a copy of the original plan for our kit house," Cassandra explained. "The night of

306

the book party, I could tell you really admired the design, and I thought you might like this, to remember the case by."

"Wow," Mallory said. "Thanks! Since I'm going to be designing a new Three Investigators Headquarters this summer, I can use this for inspiration!"

On the way to Per Jorgensen's, nobody talked much, except for Mrs. Vasiliev, who was sitting next to Bob. They were discussing the way Bob wrote up The Three Investigators cases and then posted them online. When Bob explained that he alphabetized the titles, Mrs. Vasiliev asked what title he would give the current case, and when he told her, she clapped her hands together and said, "That is *perfect*!"

She started talking about the fact that in the Soviet Union, writers and artists had known all about indefatigable ink. The regime had censored everything, and dissidents had produced unofficial literature called *samizdat*.

Although Jupiter had a lot of unexpected information stuffed inside his head, he had never heard of *samizdat* and was impressed to learn that it referred to the process by which writers and readers bypassed official publishing channels in order to communicate truthfully with one another. Since most typewriters and printing devices in the Soviet Union had required registration to access, a lot of the unauthorized and uncensored writing was actually copied manually.

"That world was a nightmare," said Mrs. Vasiliev. "But the *samizdat* writers were heroes. *Samizdat* means self-published, literally, but what it *really* means is truth!"

"I can see that," Bob said. "And that's what every writer worth the name should be trying to produce!"

It had been over ten months since Jupiter and the others had been at Per's house, but as they passed the totem pole and bounced down the rutted driveway, Jupiter thought it looked just the way it had the night The Three Investigators had caught the German con-man Günther Böhm trying to steal what he thought was a painting by the great Norwegian painter Edvard Munch.

The house's gray wooden shingles were weathered by the wind and rain off the Pacific, and the deck overlooking the ocean, with its planters of bright geraniums, was as welcoming as ever.

As Per Jorgensen came to greet them, he gestured to the side of the garage where his Jeep was now parked. "I'm glad we don't have to huddle in the woodshed again, waiting for that fraud!" he said.

With him was Brigitte, his handsome German Shepherd, and as she raced toward them, prancing and wagging her tail, it almost seemed as if she remembered them.

Pete fell to his knees and welcomed her. "Hi, girl," he said, scratching her ears.

Soon, they were all seated on the deck. Below them the Pacific sparkled as the sun started its long descent toward the horizon. Jupiter saw the steep path that led down to the beach — where Brigitte had brought down Böhm as he'd tried to escape.

To Jupiter's mild astonishment, he saw a willowy woman with long blond hair and a big straw hat coming up the path. Soon Per was introducing her. Her name was Jo March — "I know, I know," she said, when Mallory looked at her in surprise, "just like in *Little Women*. My mother loved the book, and when she married my father, she simply couldn't resist." When she took off her sunglasses, Jupiter saw that her eyes were warm and brown.

Though Jupiter had never read *Little Women*, he understood from Ms. March's comment and Mallory's response that Jo March must be its heroine. He remembered his own recent reflection about how the names they were given might affect both people and books.

Per explained that Jo was a neighbor and that she'd been a camerawoman on one of the movies he'd worked on. Jupiter couldn't tell whether she and Per were dating, but they seemed very friendly.

With her arrival, the assembled company had grown to nine – plus Brigitte – and in very short order everyone was settled with a drink as Per fired up his gas grill. He'd made potato salad and deviled eggs and Jo March had brought loaves of round Italian bread and several cheeses. There was a big green salad, small sour pickles, and crudités – which Jupiter learned was French for assorted raw vegetables served with a sauce. Per grilled hamburgers and meatless burgers, and while he was doing that, Jupiter leaned in to ask, as politely as possible, why he wanted to make a movie about the Vikings.

"What makes you interested in that subject?" he asked.

"I'm Danish, of course," Per said, "and probably descended from Vikings. But aside from that, I've always admired their boldness. Though they could be incredibly cruel, they were also curious and courageous, and they honored men and women who were good at what they did. I grew up reading sagas written by poets called skalds, and also admiring Viking metalwork. Any culture that produces both real literature and real art has something to recommend it."

"I also wondered why you called it the Viking empire the other day," Jupiter said. "It wasn't really an empire, was it?"

"Not in the way the Roman, the Ottoman, and the British empires were," Per said. "Or the Russian, Soviet, or American ones. In fact, I really shouldn't have said that. Although the Vikings had a lot of influence in the world for a couple of hundred years, they never had a centralized system of control. Though they *did* have a high opinion of themselves!" He laughed easily. "Still, all empires fail in the end. They rise and fall. What matters is that in every generation there are people who understand what it means to be free – free to speak, and think, and explore, and make."

Jupiter was glad The Three Investigators had met Per the summer before – and that, because he and Ivan had both been working on the movie about Catherine the Great, Per had been willing to help them out with the interviews of Ivan's high school classmates. He was really a very impressive person – though so was Mrs. Vasiliev, Jupiter reflected.

While they ate, Ivan and Cassandra talked some more about Ivan's grandfather's book, while Mrs. Vasiliev talked about life in the Soviet Union, and *samizdat.*

"Yes, yes," she said at one point, in response to another question from Bob. "What was so astonishing about the Soviet censors is that they censored *everything.* Not just dissident texts, but also adventure stories, science fiction and fantasy, and mystery novels. Mystery novels, if you can believe it! Of course, Vadim's novel about his parents' flight from the Bolshevik bloodbath could never have been published under the old regime, but neither could his detective fiction!"

"That's really bonkers," Mallory said.

"And science fiction and fantasy, too?" asked Bob. "I just read a fantasy written in the early 1940s and originally published in *Weird Tales.* It was called 'The Book and The Beast.' I really liked it – and in a way, it was also about indefatigable ink!"

"Hoo!" said Mrs. Vasiliev. "Yes, of *course* science fiction and fantasy! The first book banned by the Soviet censorship board was a science fiction book. In 1921, Yevgeny

Zamyatin wrote *We* – a novel set in a future world gone very wrong. A man with a number, not a name, lives in a state called the One State, where the buildings are all made of glass so that the secret police can watch people all the time. In the end, he is operated on, and his imagination and emotions are removed. You can imagine how little the Bolsheviks appreciated this portrait of themselves!

"The odd thing was, Zamyatin was the son of a Russian Orthodox priest. When he was young, he lost his faith in Christianity and became a Bolshevik himself," Mrs. Vasiliev added. "But when the revolution actually came, he couldn't stand what it was doing to the Russian people. For which reason he was blacklisted and eventually went into exile."

"I wish you'd been with us when we saw *Dawn Over Petrograd* in the film library," Pete said. "Jupiter figured out a lot of the things that Vadim's father did to protest the message of that movie, but I bet you would have figured out even more!"

"Not necessarily," Mrs. Vasiliev said. "I might have been too busy throwing up in the bathroom!"

Everyone laughed and then sat in companionable silence for a moment. Suddenly, they heard a series of hollow pops, one after the other. It sounded like gunfire. For a moment, Jupiter was startled, but then he realized that it was a celebration and not a threat or an attack. Someone on the beach was shooting off firecrackers. Soon it would be America's birthday, and he and Pete and Bob and Mallory would be going to the world premiere of Daman Duwalia's movie *Time Twist: Independence Day*.

In the movie, Daman's character traveled back in time to the day the Continental Congress had declared America's independence from Great Britain. That had been less than two hundred and fifty years ago, but a lot had changed in those years, and Jupiter wondered what the men who had signed the Declaration of Independence – and had later signed off on the First Amendment to the United States Constitution – would think of what had happened to Vadim Fedorov when he'd been accused of being a Communist. Nothing good, Jupiter imagined.

Even so, he felt very optimistic suddenly. After all, with their first three cases of the summer, The Three Investigators were on a real roll. When this case had started, he'd thought that, whatever happened, it couldn't compare to their recent triumphs. But finding a long-lost novel which told a long-buried story had actually been quite terrific.

He'd been considering the concept of treasure too literally, he thought. Priceless Medici artifacts, a telescope made by Galileo, even the Minoan hoard of gold objects and jewelry – surely all of that *was* treasure that The Three Investigators had rescued. But it was tangible and concrete and therefore, to some extent, limited in its reach.

Of course, *The Unbridled Empire* was also a physical object, as well as something bigger. And until it had been rediscovered, there'd been no way to know the worth of the manuscript pages that had gone missing.

In fact, when Jupiter had looked at the pages they'd rescued, wet with foam and touched by fire, he'd felt a little worried. Until those pages were picked up and read, they were lifeless, even meaningless. But then, through an alchemical process unlike any other, they were translated into meaning in a reader's consciousness – where they suddenly exploded into something with the power to change the world.

Now *that* was true treasure, Jupiter thought.

ABOUT THE AUTHORS

Elizabeth Arthur

Elizabeth was born on November 15, 1953 in New York City. She is the daughter of Robert Arthur, the creator of The Three Investigators series. She was educated at Concord Academy in Concord, Massachusetts, the University of Michigan in Ann Arbor, Michigan, Notre Dame University of Nelson, British Columbia, and the University of Victoria in Victoria, British Columbia.

Before she started working on the New Three Investigators series in December of 2018, Elizabeth spent most of her life writing for adults. *Island Sojourn* – a memoir about building a house on a wilderness island in northern Canada – was published in 1980 by Harper and Row. A second memoir, *Looking For The Klondike Stone,* was published by Knopf in 1992. She is also the author of the novels *Beyond the Mountain, Bad Guys, Binding Spell, Antarctic Navigation,* and *Bring Deeps.*

Elizabeth's writing has received fellowships, grants, and awards from the Bread Loaf Writer's Conference, the Ossabaw Island Project, the Vermont Council on the Arts, and the Indiana Arts Commission. She twice received fellowships from the National Endowment for the Arts and was the first novelist ever given an Antarctic Artists and Writers Operational Support Grant from the National Science Foundation.

Her novel *Antarctic Navigation* was chosen by the New York *Times* as a Notable Book, received a Critics' Choice Award from the San Francisco *Review of Books*, and was chosen as a Best Book of 1995 by *A Common Reader*. In 1996 the novel received the Ohioana Book Award for Fiction from the Ohioana Library Association.

Elizabeth has also taught creative writing at Miami University in Oxford, Ohio; the University of Cincinnati; and Indiana University/Purdue University of Indianapolis, where she directed the creative writing program. She and Steven Bauer met in 1980 at the Bread Loaf Writer's Conference and have been married since June of 1982.

Steven Bauer

Steven was born on September 10, 1948 in Newark, New Jersey. He was educated at Hanover Park High School in East Hanover, New Jersey, Trinity College in Hartford, Connecticut, and the University of Massachusetts in Amherst, Massachusetts. In 1970 he received a B.A. with Honors in English from Trinity, and in 1975 he received an M.F.A. in English from the University of Massachusetts.

Steven is the author of three books for young people – *Satyrday*, 1980; *The Strange and Wonderful Tale of Robert McDoodle*, 1999; and *A Cat of a Different Color*, 2000. His book of poems *Daylight Savings* was published by Gibbs Smith in 1989 and won the Peregrine Smith Poetry Prize.

Steven's work has received fellowships from the Bread Loaf Writer's Conference and the Fine Arts Work Center in Provincetown, Massachusetts. In addition, he has been given grants and awards from the American Library Association, the Parents' Choice Foundation, the Ossabaw Island Project, the Massachusetts Arts Council, and the Indiana Arts Commission.

From 1979 to 1982, Steven taught literature and creative writing at Colby College in Waterville, Maine. From 1982 to 2009 he taught at Miami University in Oxford, Ohio where he directed the graduate and under-graduate creative writing programs. In 2010 he established Hollow Tree Literary Services, an independent editing business.